SIX WAYS TO SUNDAY

CHRISTIAN McPHERSON

Six
ways to
Sunday

NIGHTWOOD EDITIONS
Gibsons Landing, BC

Published by Nightwood Editions
773 Cascade Crescent
Gibsons, BC, Canada V0N 1V9
www.nightwoodeditions.com

Author photo by Judith Gustafsson
Cover design by Anna Comfort
Printed and bound in Canada

Nightwood Editions acknowledges financial support from the Government of Canada through the Canada Council for the Arts and the Book Publishing Industry Development Program (BPIDP), and from the Province of British Columbia through the British Columbia Arts Council, for its publishing activities.

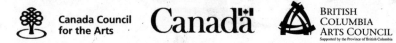

Library and Archives Canada Cataloguing in Publication

McPherson, Christian
    Six ways to Sunday / Christian McPherson.

ISBN 978-0-88971-227-0

    I. Title.

PS8625.P53S59 2007   C813'.6   C2007-901473-9

CONTENTS

For beautiful Marty

THE PLASTIC GARDEN

Rumford found that dental clay worked best. He had tried different modelling clays and wall fillers, but after a time they would crack, or even worse crumble. The tip about the dental clay had come from an exquisite castle builder at the "Models and Miniatures Fair" in Toronto. After that, Rumford never looked back.

Dental clay, normally used by dentists for casting teeth, was quite expensive. But Rumford had lots of money. He didn't drink. He didn't smoke. He didn't dine out. The one thing he never skimped on though, was his passion—his models.

When Rumford was ten, his Uncle Larry bought him his first model—a balsa wood replica of an 1886 sailing ship, *The Scottish Mermaid*. It had taken Rumford six months to build, and he loved every minute of it. After that, he was hooked. He built everything he could get his hands on. Ships, planes, cars, tanks; it didn't matter. If it were a model and it looked challenging, Rumford bought it and built it.

Rumford was very bright and had been blessed with the rare gift of patience; the kind ascetic monks have, who can spend twenty years carving a single cross. Maybe this was the reason Rumford didn't get along with the other kids at school. They were all too animated. Too loud. Too stupid.

He preferred the company of books to people. He liked history and mathematics. He liked studying about the things he built. When he wasn't studying, he was building, and when he wasn't building, he was studying. People were boring.

The only kid Rumford found remotely interesting was David Fern. David liked to build cranes and winches that used complex pulley systems. Sometimes David would invite Rumford over after school to help him work on a new crane design. But for the most part, Rumford kept to himself.

It was in the first few months of grade six that Rumford had learned a valuable lesson about humanity. He brought in a model of a German U-boat for a class presentation on World War One. He had worked on the model for months, and it was one of his favourites. During the afternoon's recess, Rumford found his precious German U-boat in enemy territory, namely the greasy hands of the class bully, Vince Gamble. Rumford watched in horror as Vince put the U-boat afloat on the calm waters of a toilet bowl in the boys' washroom. Vince lit the two cherry bombs he had strapped to the U-boat's hull and blew the Germans out of the water, so to speak.

The real horror for Rumford wasn't the loss of the boat, but rather the realization that there are two kinds of people in the world: those who are builders, and those who are destroyers. Vince Gamble was definitely a destroyer.

The summer before Rumford started university, Rumford went to London, England to live with his grandmother. She took him to see all the sights of the city including the Tower of London and St. Paul's Cathedral. Rumford was completely smitten with these English landmarks, so much so that after completing his BA he went on to do an MA in History, specializing in architectural history.

During university he landed a summer job at a large architectural firm building models of houses and skyscrapers. He loved it so much and did such a brilliant job that after finishing school Rumford was offered a full-time job by Northwood Architecture. He built models for them for almost forty years. But with the development of CAD systems and 3-D virtual reality tours, Rumford's job became obsolete.

So on the insistence of the company, Rumford took early retirement. Rumford didn't want to leave, as work was the only social interaction he had with people outside of the grocery store and McFee's Model Shop. Not that Rumford had come to really like people all that much, but he had come to enjoy the rhythms of the office. It was the regularity with which the office moved, everyone a piece of a complicated clock—moving, meeting, talking, eating—all in step with one another.

Now Rumford was home, retired, with nobody to watch and no rhythms to follow. But that was okay. Now he could devote all his time to building *his* models. Rumford had spent the last eight years building a replica of St. Paul's Cathedral. It had a removable dome and stood almost six feet high. He spent two years alone replicating the intricate stained-glass windows of the cathedral. Thousands and thousands of hours logged squinting through a monocle, manipulating the tiniest pieces of thin plastic with tweezers, gluing them together. The level of detail was incredible. He had made four trips to London to photograph and study the cathedral. Every statue, every pew, every tomb, was meticulously recorded and rebuilt on a smaller scale. Rumford's model was a thing of beauty.

The Tower of London was next. Millions of stones and bricks were going to have to be made. To date Rumford had made seventy-five moulds for the different types of stonework that he was going to use in the Tower's outer wall. He kept the moulds in several old wooden card-catalogue cabinets that he had found abandoned beside a dumpster. The cabinet drawers were carefully labelled and cross-referenced in a large binder so Rumford could tell which moulds were used to make which section of any given wall.

The Tower of London had taken over the entire expanse of Rumford's dining room. Would Mother have approved of building such a monstrosity on her dining room table? Definitely not. Rumford smiled at the thought, but she was long gone. He had been in this house, by himself, for a very long time. His father had died when he was only a small child. Car crash. His mother had died shortly after he finished university. Heart attack.

Rumford was gluing a section of the wall when he heard beeps and felt the rumbling of a large truck. He looked out the window to see a moving truck backing into the laneway across the street. Rumford turned back and resumed his work.

......

The milk in the refrigerator had expired. Rumford had been in a frenzied pattern of building, like that of a junkie or an alcoholic on a binge. He'd been working on the Tower for over eighteen hours straight. When he finally realized that he should eat something, he watched sour milk curdle on his Frosted

Flakes. He didn't have anything else in the cupboards to eat. Rumford surmised it was time for an adventure to the corner store. When was the last time he had been out? Must have been over three days ago. So he showered, trimmed his beard, and put on a fresh short sleeved shirt, his favourite red and green plaid bowtie, cotton slacks, and his Birkenstock sandals.

Just before leaving, Rumford noticed the small pile of mail that had accumulated under the slot of the front door. Amongst the assorted bills, pizza flyers and grocery store advertisements, Rumford was quite happy to find his latest copy of *Model Railroader*. Although Rumford was not all that interested in model trains, over the years the magazine had provided interesting techniques on landscaping. Rumford had even written a few articles for them, such as creative and easy ways to make miniature trees and shrubbery from copper wire and foam rubber.

On his way back from the store, the plastic bag handles looped around Rumford's arm made red imprints on his flesh. Despite being weighed down with a tin of coffee, a carton of milk and twelve cans of Zoodles, Rumford employed a one-armed reading technique to continue reading his magazine. Rumford awkwardly continued shifting the bags, as if by moving them around on his arm they would somehow become lighter. Close to home, his nose was deeply buried in an article on lighting model houses.

"Hello there," boomed a voice on Rumford's immediate right. Rumford jumped slightly.

"Sorry, didn't mean to startle you," said the voice. "I'm your new neighbour Jackson—Paul Jackson."

Rumford turned to see a man holding a garden hose in his

driveway. Behind him was a soapy car. Rumford had been so engrossed in his magazine that he would have walked by his own house had it not been for this interruption.

"Paul Jackson," said the man, extending his hand.

As Rumford tried to shake it, one of the plastic bags slipped down the length of his arm and spit out a can of Zoodles. "Oh my," said Rumford, and as he bent down to retrieve the runaway can two more tins jumped out.

Paul watched as Rumford comically tried to capture the escaped Zoodles. Whenever he would put a can into the bag and attempt to pick up another one, the first one would fly back out. Eventually, after several attempts, Paul came to Rumford's aid and they quickly snared the lot.

"My daughter Haley likes these too," said Paul, as he placed the last can of Zoodles back into one of Rumford's many plastic bags.

"Thanks so much, very sorry about that. Haven't been shopping for a while. Don't know where all the time goes," said Rumford with a nervous chuckle.

"That's Haley there," said Paul, pointing to a little girl in a yellow and white flowered dress. She was playing with a plastic turtle amongst the flowers of the garden in the front yard.

"Oh yes," said Rumford and smiled.

Rumford looked at Haley and then at the garden of flowers that stretched down from the house and wound their way along the footpath to the curb. Tiny faces were staring at Rumford—horses, gorillas, bears, giraffes, wolves and more. Scattered throughout the flowers were little plastic animals.

"Oh look at all the animals," exclaimed Rumford.

"You've got a nice eye for detail. Most people don't notice them unless they look really carefully."

"Oh," said Rumford as he continued to look.

Haley ran down and stood before Rumford with her arm stretched out, palm up.

"This is my turtle Ernie, wanna see?" asked Haley.

"Oh yes," said Rumford, bending closer to take a better look.

"It's not real, it's just plastic. These are all my animals," said Haley, pointing and spinning around.

Rumford straightened up and continued to smile. Haley went over and hung on to her daddy's leg.

"Listen, unless you are really set on eating Zoodles, why don't you join us for a barbecue?" asked Paul.

"Well, I should really get back to work."

"It's Saturday, you shouldn't be working on a Saturday. Besides, June, my wife, would love some company. Come on, whaddya say?"

"Well I don't want to be any bother."

"No bother, we would love to have you. Why don't you stop around in a couple of hours? Listen, I never did catch your name?"

"It's Rumford, Rumford Bendell, and I live across the street."

......

The little creatures seemed right at home with one another: penguins living next to lions, cows living next to hippos, alligators living next to polar bears, and all of them living amongst the peach and purple flowers lining the footpath to the Jacksons' front door. With his spidery index finger, Rumford gingerly pushed the doorbell and waited. He noticed Ernie the turtle had been returned to his designated spot in the soil. Rumford liked the order of it, the detail.

The door swung open and there stood a beautiful smiling woman with thick blonde hair that fell to her shoulders.

"You must be Rumford," she said. "I'm June, Paul's wife."

Rumford held up a six-pack of Coors Light as if it were a dead rat he had found in the basement and said, "Silver bullets."

"Well you shouldn't have," said June laughing and taking the beer. "Come on in. Paul and Haley are playing in the backyard. Don't bother to take your shoes off. Follow me."

They moved through the house which was neat and clean. It looked the way his mother would have kept it.

"Beer?" asked June as they arrived in the kitchen.

"Umm, no thanks, I don't really drink," said Rumford.

"Well I'm going to have one. You sure, you never drink?"

"Well sometimes."

"So you want one?"

"Okay."

"Glass?"

"No thanks, the can will be fine."

The patio door slid open and Paul emerged from the backyard.

"Hey Rumford, I thought I heard the doorbell. I see you got a beer. I'll take one of those," said Paul as he ripped a beer out of the plastic holder, popped it open and drained half of it.

"Ha, hoooo weeee," exclaimed Paul catching his breath. "Man it's sure hot out there."

Rumford noticed Paul was sweating. He was a big man,

strong, good looking. He was the kind of guy Rumford normally wouldn't like. But there was something different about Paul, a gentleness. Most people wouldn't have invited Rumford for a barbecue. But Paul did, without knowing anything about him. Just like that. Like the way he just grabbed a beer and drank it down. Just like that.

......

They were all sitting under the white and green umbrella of a backyard patio set about to dine on T-bone steaks and potato salad. Rumford was feeling light-headed and rather giddy after his third beer. He hadn't slept in over twenty hours. So when June asked him what he did for a living, Rumford sat up straight and proudly answered in a booming 1950s movie superhero voice that he built models.

"What kind of models?" asked June, laughing.

"Errr well, I used to build models for an architectural firm but I retired last year."

"So what do you do now, I mean to keep yourself busy that is?"

"Well actually I still build models, only they are ones that I really want to work on."

"Can you make me a kangaroo?" asked Haley.

"Hey Haley, it's not polite to ask people for things," said Paul as he cut the steak on her plate into little pieces.

"That's okay, I probably could. I've made practically everything else in my life."

"Have you made a bluebird?" asked Haley as she popped a piece of meat into her mouth.

"No, never a bluebird. I've never built any animals before, but maybe I'll give it a try."

"What are you working on now, Rumford?" asked Paul.

"The Tower of London. You should come over and see it sometime."

"Sounds like a plan," said Paul.

"Maybe after dinner?" asked Rumford. Just like that.

"Okay, we'll go after dinner," said Paul.

"After dessert," said June. "I made apple pie."

......

Each step across the street was sobering. The only other person who had seen the inside of Rumford's home in the last twenty years, besides Rumford, was the pizza delivery guy—and he had only seen the hallway.

Rumford fumbled for his keys.

"Ahh, I must warn you that my place is rather messy. I'm not used to having guests," said Rumford, visibly shaking as he attempted to open the front door.

Paul placed a hand on his shoulder and told him it was okay, not to worry. A wave of calm enveloped Rumford and he instantly felt better.

The smell of model glue and paint was the first thing to greet the Jackson family.

"It stinks in here," said Haley.

"Don't say *stinks* baby, it's not nice," said June.

Rumford ran ahead, turning on lights, telling them to come on in. After the smell, it was the walls they noticed next. The hallways, the living room, the dining room and parts of the ceiling were covered in architectural maps and drawings and photos of St. Paul's Cathedral and the Tower of London. Crazy, thought June, simply crazy.

As they moved further into the living room, June was the first one to see it. Her mouth popped open in disbelief.

"Wow," said June.

There, standing almost six feet tall, was the most impressive model she had ever seen in her life—St. Paul's Cathedral. An exact copy, only smaller.

"Holy cow," said Paul.

"Do mice live in there?" asked Haley.

"I hope not," answered Rumford, closely watching the reaction of Haley's parents to his work.

"Wow," repeated June. "I cannot get over it. Look at the detail. It's truly amazing, Rumford."

"It's stunning, Rumford," said Paul.

"Well, it's really nothing," said Rumford.

"Modesty in this particular case would be rather silly, no?" asked Paul.

"Perhaps," said Rumford with a smile. He was drunk and happy. The Jacksons were the first outsiders ever to lay eyes on his personal work. He was happy it was them. He was happy it was spontaneous—just like that.

They were full of questions, so Rumford showed them everything—the moulds, the cabinets, where he worked, how he worked. He even showed them how he cast miniature bricks with dental clay.

As he hopped into bed that night he imagined himself as one of the kings of England, lying peacefully in a crypt in the bowels of St. Paul's. He fell asleep quickly.

......

Crash. Clack clack clack. Smash!

Rumford awoke suddenly. He looked over and saw the red glow of *3:04 a.m.* Laughter and yelling and a clack clack clacking were coming from outside his window. He swung his feet to the floor and brushed back the curtains. In the middle of the street a kid was doing multiple three-sixties while adeptly holding a bottle of beer. There were a couple of other kids leaning up against a car, smoking and drinking and cheering on their buddy until the skateboard flew out from under him and he landed on his ass, then they roared with laughter. Another kid came clack clack clacking along the sidewalk. He stopped in the middle of the street to try his own trick, a trick requiring sober navigation. Laughter and scraped elbows always seemed to ensue.

They were slowing making their way down the street, presumably to the park where they could further injure themselves on more substantial equipment than a bare asphalt road. Rumford would have normally just let them move on, but one of the kids noticed the plastic garden. A boy spotted a giraffe sticking out of the flowers. He picked it up.

"Hey guys, check it out, a giraffe!" yelled the boy.

"Here give it to me," said a second boy. He grabbed it, took out a lighter from his pocket and melted the head of the animal.

The two boys watched as the long neck of the animal dripped off its body like gooey taffy.

"Is that cool or what?"

"Totally awesome. Hey, there is a whole bunch more. Let's

melt them all together. We can make like Greek gods and shit. You know, put a lion's head on the body of a goat and shit like that."

"Come on you idiots, forget the animals, let's get to the park. Josh, gimme your backpack, I want another beer."

Josh stood up, his backpack clinking with the sound of bottles, his arms full of plastic animals and a half finished beer. The flowers were crushed where Josh had meandered through the bed.

"Here Tommy, melt these together while I get Sean a brewski."

"Come on, take 'em to the park before someone comes out of the house."

One of the boys was still in the middle of the street trying to perform a kick-flip move when he caught sight of the elderly man in plaid pyjamas coming across the street.

"Guys, let's go *now!*" yelled the boy.

They all turned and saw Rumford coming across the street at them.

"Put those down," said Rumford. "They don't belong to you. Why are you destroying things?"

Sean, a tall good-looking kid and obviously the leader of the bunch, stepped in front of Rumford.

"Go fuck yourself old dude," slurred Sean as he took a swig of his beer.

"Put those animals back," ordered Rumford again.

Tommy continued to melt the animals.

"What are you gonna do about it old man?" demanded Sean as he poked Rumford in the chest.

And Rumford didn't know. He thought of grabbing the boy and shaking him, but to what avail? What should he do?

He was nervous. He was about to say something when the door of the Jackson house opened and Paul stepped out into the moonlight wearing only his boxers.

Tommy dropped the animals.

"Let's go!" yelled Sean.

"The police are on their way, you little bastards!" yelled Paul.

All four boys grabbed their boards and threw them to the ground and took off.

"Fuck you!" Sean yelled back as he threw his beer bottle over his shoulder. It smashed a few feet in front of Rumford as he was reaching down to pick up the melted giraffe.

"Ahhh," said Rumford as he covered his right eye with the palm of his hand.

"You okay?" asked Paul as he came over to where Rumford was standing.

"I think I got a shard of glass in the eye."

"Come in the house and let June take a look."

"Okay," said Rumford softly.

June appeared in the door holding Haley.

"Mommy, look, they took Ernie!" screamed Haley pointing down to an empty patch of dirt next to a crushed flower.

"Don't worry baby, we will find him," said June.

"Mommy Mommy, they took my Ernie," sobbed Haley.

Rumford noticed the half-melted plastic turtle by the curb and picked it up. He slipped it into his shirt pocket before Haley noticed it.

......

After flushing his eye in the Jacksons' sink, and making a statement to the police, Rumford was chauffeured by Paul to the hospital. Rumford underwent an eye dye test that revealed a scratched cornea. He was going to have to wear a patch on his right eye for a week. It was 7:30 a.m. by the time they finally got home. Rumford thanked Paul for the ride. Paul said not to mention it.

Rumford went to his bedroom, changed back into his pyjamas, and lay down on the bed. He took the melted turtle and looked it over. He put it on the nightstand next to his watch. Why didn't he shake the kid, scare him a little? *Hey go fuck yourself old dude? Go fuck yourself. Oh yeah, you little destroying shit, grab you by the scruff of your baggy shirt and give you a good shake. Now they know I mean business! Ha! And that's when the kid reaches for his pocket knife, and that's when I grab his arm with one hand and slap him across the face with the other. Take that you little shit, you should have some respect for your elders. Ha! Pick up the knife the kid dropped and hold it up to his throat. Leave now and never come back here or I'll cut your worthless heart out, you little cheeky bastard.*

Rumford lay on his back with his fists clenched and his heart racing, reliving the scene, doing what he would have liked to have done. His ears were hot and his eye pulsed under the bandage. He kept going over it, replaying it in his mind, over and over.

With the combination of adrenalin and anger, and the sun coming into the room brightly, Rumford couldn't sleep. He got up and went downstairs with the charred plastic turtle carcass. He placed it gingerly on his workbench with the other four animals that Paul had found melted. A trip to the library was required. Anatomical proportions, colouring, and proper shape must all be maintained. Rumford was going to need several picture books.

By 10 p.m. the moulds for the giraffe and the bear were beginning to dry and Rumford was putting the final touches on Ernie's new shell. After letting the paint dry for a couple of hours, Rumford crossed the dark street and placed the new Ernie in his old terrestrial spot in the garden. He smiled at his work. He turned to leave when he remembered.

"Almost forgot," said Rumford as he laid a little business card beside the turtle that read: "Courtesy of the Magic Garden Fairy."

The smile was burned into Rumford's face as he drifted off to sleep that night. He kept thinking about what Haley's expression would be when she saw that Ernie was back, alive and well.

......

Over the next few nights the Magic Garden Fairy restored beautifully painted, beautifully detailed, dental clay replicas of the burned plastic animals. When the patch was taken off of Rumford's eye, June and Paul had Rumford over for dinner to thank him. They told him how happy he had made Haley. Rumford told them that it was nothing, that in fact he really liked making them. And the truth was, Rumford loved making them.

After the animals had been repaired, the Magic Garden Fairy's imagination burst with creativity. New exotic four-inch additions started to appear once a week; a peacock, an orang-utan, a great blue whale, a unicorn and a brontosaurus. Rumford found carving the tiny little animals a wonderful distraction from the ominous task of completing the Tower of London.

Rumford got lost in the details. There was so much fine detail in each of the animals, the gradational changes in the grain of the fur, the skin and the feathers; the way texture changed along the body of any given animal.

At night he would fall asleep thinking about the plastic garden, about the wondrous creatures that inhabited it, about what he could make next. Maybe a tarantula? No, too scary for little Haley. A skunk? Yes, that would be fun, thought Rumford, a skunk it would be.

As he lay awake thinking about how to design the stinky beast, Rumford heard the sound. Immediately his heart beat faster, his palms perspired. The clack, clack, clacking was coming down the road. The skateboarder kids were back. It had been almost two months since the incident.

Rumford swung himself out of bed, ran to the other room and returned holding an old pair of binoculars. He raised them to his face and looked out the window, focussing on the Jacksons' garden across the street. He could make out the head of the brontosaurus majestically sticking up through the petunias. He removed the glasses from his eyes.

Outside the familiar faces of the skateboarders were coming down the road. He saw the first one go by, then the second, then the third. Rumford prayed they wouldn't notice, wouldn't stop. *Move on, that's it, keep going you little buggers, keep it going, keep it moving along.* But the fourth kid was on the sidewalk, looking down at the flowers when he went zooming by the Jacksons' house. The kid stopped his board.

"Hey, check it out guys, it's that house with those animals, where the old guy came out and gave us shit," said the kid.

The kid picked up the brontosaurus and felt the weight of it in his hand.

"Hey, this one isn't plastic," said the kid as he whipped it at the ground.

The brontosaurus smashed to bits on the sidewalk.

"Smash 'em all, teach 'em a lesson. Dumb fools shouldn't put out this stuff, kids just come along and break it," said Sean.

All the kids laughed.

The kid in the flowers grabbed the great blue whale and threw it into the middle of the street where it smashed into fat chunks of clay.

They all heard the door open and saw the same old man running out again from his house wearing the same silly plaid pyjamas.

"Stop!" yelled Rumford. "Stop that!"

One kid went to grab another animal. The leader of the group stepped in front of Rumford as he was crossing the street. Rumford was the boy's senior by five inches in height, and fifty-five years in age.

"Where do you think you're going Grandpa?" asked the leader as he placed his palm on Rumford's chest.

Rumford slapped the boy's hand away.

"You have no right to go around breaking things, destroying things," said Rumford.

The peacock came flying threw the air and smashed by Rumford's right foot.

"Go back home old man," said one of the boys.

Rumford felt the blood rise into his face, felt the pulsing in his ears. He clenched his fists.

The leader gave Rumford a good shove and ordered him to go home. Rumford fell backwards on the ground. The other kids were laughing. The smell of burning paint came down from the lawn. In the flowers a kid was laughing as he melted the ass of a plastic polar bear.

Rumford stood up and grabbed the leader by the throat with his left hand. The boy's eyes widened in surprise. Rumford's long bony fingers coiled around the boy's neck like a boa constrictor. They tightened.

The boy's mouth opened and his tongue came out, but no sound. The boy tried to pull Rumford's hand off, but the fingers were locked. Rumford watched as the boy's face turned red and his eyes turned in desperation to his friends for help. But none came. The other kids didn't move. They looked scared. They even backed up a little, like they were prepared to run.

In desperation the boy started swinging punches at Rumford. Rumford dodged them as he continued to squeeze the boy's throat. Finally the boy landed a solid punch in Rumford's gut and sent him to the ground winded. Rumford clutched at his stomach, trying desperately to catch his breath. The boy was bent over, hands on his knees trying to do the same thing. The boy sucked in big gulps of air that sounded like a clogged sink that was finally clearing.

"You okay Sean?" asked one of the boys.

Sean coughed and croaked out that he was. Then he saw the old man struggling on the ground, arms wrapped around his abdomen. Sean ran and kicked Rumford in the gut. Rumford let out a sound like a tire leaking air.

"That's it Sean, get that old fucker, teach him a lesson for calling the cops on us!" yelled one of the kids.

Rumford couldn't catch his breath, couldn't call out for help. The smell of burning plastic was in his nose. The disembodied eye of the great blue whale stared up at Rumford from the ground as he felt himself get kicked again, this time in the shoulder.

It was then that Rumford caught a good full breath. He caught it just in time to see Sean's foot coming at him again. Rumford managed to dodge the boy's kick and grab him by the ankle. Rumford stood up, still holding the boy's ankle. The boy fell backwards.

Rumford knelt down and the snake-like fingers of his left hand quickly slid back around the boy's throat and tightened. Sean's mouth reopened and his tongue came popping out like an eel out of its cave.

The difference this time was Rumford was kneeling on the boy's chest. Rumford looked up and around at the other boys. They all backed up. Sean struggled and squirmed beneath Rumford. Rumford's eyes welled with tears as he raised his right fist in the air.

He brought it down on the boy, brought it down with rage, the rage of seventy years. He brought it up and down again. And again. And again. And again. Rumford got lost in the movement of the teeth, the muscles and shape of the face. Despite the blood, the bubbles, and its sheen in the streetlight, the fusion of flesh and bone was so basic, so easy to manipulate. His hand kept going up and down.

He heard the screams of a woman. It was June. She was yelling, screaming his name, screaming for him to stop, but

Rumford couldn't understand it. His own heartbeat was in his head, in his ears. It muted everything.

His hand came down again one last time into the pulpy mess before Rumford was finally pulled off by Paul Jackson.

"Rumford!" yelled Paul.

Rumford stared at his bloody clenched fist.

"Rumford, say something!" Paul commanded.

Rumford looked at Paul with his blood-splattered face, looked at him for a good long time and finally said, "I'm sorry."

Somewhere in the background they heard the long sharp wail of sirens.

LUCIFER'S TAVERN

In the summer of 1985, Lucifer's Tavern was where we grew up, where we became men. A Lebanese family ran the joint. The father or son would usually tend bar, while the wife, a big woman whom everyone called Momma, ran the restaurant section pretty much single-handedly—or so I thought at the beginning of the summer.

Momma wore an expansive platinum blonde wig and had watermelon-like breasts that spilled out of her black dress that looked more like a slinky piece of negligee. She wore a red shawl with pink flowers that covered her plump oatmeal shoulders. The shawl matched her gaudy pink lipstick and the red rouge clown-like circles on her pasty cheeks. She looked more like a whorehouse madam than a restaurant hostess.

You see I was stoned or drunk out of my mind the few times I had been to Lucifer's Tavern before. On this particular visit I had just smoked a spliff with Two Seconds and Toby, in the Paranoid Parking Lot (the five-storey parking garage around the corner) before we walked into the place.

There before my stoned self was not just Momma, but Momma and Momma. Identical twins. And I mean identical— from the platinum wig right down to the pancake makeup. I freaked out.

"Squid man, what's wrong with you, quit staring will you," said Two Seconds, jabbing me in the ribs.

"There's two of them," I eked out.

"Didn't you know they was twins?" asked Two Seconds laughing.

"Wow," was all I could muster.

We grabbed a table near the front, close to the glowing blue jukebox, which emitted just enough light to illuminate the ghostly face of some of the local patrons, like Laughing Lydia.

Lydia was an old woman who always wore this ratty fur coat with a dead fox around the collar, even in the summer. She dolled herself up with thick lipstick and heavy eye make-up, like the Mommas, but she was really thin and didn't seem to have any teeth. Lydia was a permanent fixture of the place. She was always sitting in the dark corner smacking her gums together while she worked on sucking back her mini pitchers of Molson Export draft. Occasionally she would let out a small burst of laughter as if an invisible ghost were whispering jokes in her ear. She never spoke. She would just nod yes or shake no when Momma or Momma asked her if she wanted another pitcher of beer.

Then there were Ned and Larry. These two guys were the local rummies who worked Bank Street begging for change; Ned one block north of Lucifer's Tavern, and Larry one block to the south. When they scrounged up enough, they would come into the dark of the bar and shower their table with a dancing spray of pennies, nickels, dimes and quarters. Then they would sit down and count out their loot, making sure they had four and a half bucks for a mini pitcher.

On this particular trip into the tavern, I met Gloria. She was sitting in the dark nursing a rum and coke as we piled into chairs at the next table. Two Seconds, with his displaced-decade afro and *Star Wars* T-shirt, immediately got back up, almost performing a break-dance move, and fed quarters into the starved jukebox to play the machine's only jazz album, *Kind of Blue* by Miles Davis.

"Hey cutie pie, wanna buy me a drink?" asked Gloria as she lightly tapped me on the shoulder.

"Who's that, Sid Vicious?" I asked, pointing to the tattoo on her shoulder, avoiding the drink question.

Gloria tilted her arm, glancing down at the tattoo. "Yeah," she replied, "nobody ever gets it right. They all think it's Billy Idol or Elvis."

"Well it looks just like him," I said, staring at Gloria's blue bra strap sticking out from her tight pink tank top.

"You're cute," she said picking up her drink, taking a little sip, all the time keeping her eyes on me.

Gloria had spiked black hair with red tips, like a porcupine that had been dipped in blood. The spiked leather choker, hooped earrings, black lipstick, tight black skirt, ripped fishnets and black boots gave her the look of a gothic Cyndi Lauper. I found her totally bitchin' hot.

Like I mentioned earlier, I was stoned. Speech was not flowing freely. In addition to this, girls, women, especially ones exhibiting the sexual prowess that Gloria embodied, froze me up. So in response to her exclamation that I was cute, all I could muster was, "Wow."

At this, Gloria's lips curled up at either end and I thought I heard her purr.

"Are you a hooker?" Toby blurted out.

Toby, with his Jimmy Page mop of curls and leather jacket. I wanted to smack him across the head. He was a rich kid with a big mouth. Two Seconds lived down near where Chinatown and Little Italy intersected and I lived in working-class Vanier, but Toby, well he lived in the Glebe. His father was a lawyer and his mother spent her days at the country club drinking martinis and playing tennis.

Gloria continued to smile at me like she hadn't even heard Toby, but she had. She grabbed a smoke from her pack and asked me for a light.

I fumbled out my Zippo and with a well-practised motion snapped it aflame.

"Thanks," said Gloria, exhaling smoke in Toby's face.

I heard Two Seconds snicker.

One of the Mommas came over.

"Jug of draft?"

"Yeah, and whatever this lady is drinking here," said Toby, thumbing at Gloria, waving away the smoke.

Gloria raised her glass and gave a slight nod toward Toby, barely acknowledging his existence.

Momma bent down low toward the table, whispering to the three of us that if the cops were to come in we were to move to the back and go out through the kitchen.

"No worries Momma," Two Seconds assured her. "First sign of trouble and we're gone."

"You good boys," whispered Momma in her Arabic accent, giving us a wink and Toby a pat on the arm.

"Hey, look, I'm sorry," said Toby, trying to get Gloria's attention.

34

She finally looked over at him.

"Don't worry about it, you couldn't afford me anyway," said Gloria with a big sexy smile.

We all laughed.

"So what do you really do then?" asked Toby.

"I'm a dancer next door."

"So you're a stripper then?"

"Yes. You little boys ever seen a naked girl before?"

I had never seen a naked woman, expect on rare occasions when I had seen my mother changing into her swimsuit at the beach. I had read plenty of nudie mags mind you, but up until this point I had never seen a full-fledged woman in the buff before; and boy oh boy did I ever want to.

"Sure have, my girlfriend," said Toby brimming with confidence.

"How 'bout you?" Gloria asked of Two Seconds.

"Who me?" replied Two Seconds.

"Watch your beer," said Gloria

"What? Oh shit!" realized Two Seconds as he overfilled his glass.

"And you?"

I felt hot and flustered. The dope made me honest, though. "I'm a virgin," I replied.

At that moment the front door of Lucifer's burst open, flooding the place with summer sunlight, a fireball from hell, causing everyone to squint like vampires. Through the gateway, from cars and noise, the cyclists and Saturday shoppers, passed the shadowy outline of Ned, slightly hunched, hands cupped like he was carrying a fragile egg. He found his usual table next to Lydia and splashed down a shower of panhandled coins.

One of the Mommas immediately came over and helped Ned count out his change.

"So, what's your name, virgin?" Gloria asked.

"I'm Ryan, but everyone calls me Squid," I said, offering my hand.

"I'm Gloria," said Gloria, taking my hand and squeezing ever so softly. "Why do they call you Squid?"

"Cause he smells like a dirty fish," chimed Toby.

"Cause I used to work in a fish store," I quickly explained.

"I'm Toby, and that's Two Seconds," said Toby.

"Pleased to meet you boys," said Gloria, raising up her glass in salutation and then draining it.

We spent the next few hours drinking and talking. Gloria was full of sarcasm and bitter ironies that you could almost see moving behind her pale skin, like a shadow moving behind a curtain.

Gloria told crazy tales of her life—the club, the coke, the men. She would go to Lucifer's Tavern to come down with Cuba libres until she was drunk enough to go to bed sometime in the late afternoon, get some rest before working the zombie shift at the strip club. She was halfway to nighty-night.

After a while Two Seconds pulled out his Ziploc of grass and rolled another joint right there at the table. When he was done, Gloria suggested we all go back to her place to smoke it. So we polished off our drinks and left.

Gloria lived only a block away in an eight-storey, suitably named "high-rise." The place was a giant cocaine saltshaker, peppered with cockroaches, drunks and the occasional out-of-fashion heroin junkie.

"Come on in boys," said Gloria jiggling her key in the lock, smashing the door open with a well-practised shoulder check. We followed her in.

When I walked into Gloria's tiny apartment my first thought was, *Wow, this girl is an artist.* Her pad was decorated with eclectic items obviously salvaged from the garbage: a shopping cart holding a turntable and speakers, a mannequin dressed like a nun, a coffee table in the shape of a coffin, a large wall unit containing TVs of all different sizes, and three strange lamp lights with bases made from old vacuum cleaners and topped with purple and red shades. On the walls were paintings: primarily haunting portraits of old men and women who looked liked they had seen better times.

"Wow, did you paint all of these?" I asked.

"Those, yeah. Make yourself at home boys. Who needs a beer?" asked Gloria, as she opened the fridge and fired out cans to all of us.

"Thanks," said Toby doing a one-arm catch.

"Cool place," said Two Seconds, popping open his beer.

"Very cool. You painted *all* of these?" I asked again.

"Yeah, you like 'em? Toby, spark up that doobage will yah. I've been painting for a while now. Thought about going to art school."

"You should go, you're really good," I said.

Toby lit the joint, took three big gulps of smoke, and passed it to Gloria. She took it delicately in her fingers and smoked it as if it were a cigarette. She looked at me. I fell into her black eyes in a vertigo trance.

"Wanna shotgun?" said asked me, giving a sly smile and a wink.

"Okay," is all I could muster.

Gloria took a long drag, flipped the joint around and popped the lit end into her mouth. She walked up to me, her sensuous lips pursed around the little circle of the joint's matchbook cardboard filter. A vapour of marijuana smoke snaked from her cauldron lips, dangerous and beckoning. I exhaled all the air I had, put my lips to hers and inhaled slowly. Before being overwhelmed with smoke, our lips touched. I felt my adolescent crotch burn with desire. I pulled away and fought to keep the smoke in, making clucking sounds within my throat.

Gloria pulled the joint from her mouth and passed it to Two Seconds. She drifted over to the shopping cart and put on a record from a band called Soft Cell. I took a seat on the retro '60s couch. Gloria came and sat beside me and threw an arm around my shoulder.

She could see I was nervous and this seemed to excite her. She leaned in and gave me a peck on the cheek, much like a grandmother would, only a bit softer and much longer. I blushed uncontrollably. Two Seconds and Toby were grinning enviously at me. I had only ever kissed one girl before. Now here I was, in a gorgeous stripper's apartment, high to the gills. I was living out the fantasy of most adolescent men.

We smoked a few more joints and Gloria continued to play freaky UK bands on her shopping cart hi-fi. My attention was split between Gloria's fishnets and a painting on the wall of an old man with a bulbous, alcoholic nose and sad blue eyes. I got lost in the strokes of paint, in his nose, and in his eyes.

The next thing I knew Toby was slapping Two Seconds and saying they should get going.

"Ahh, alright," said Two Seconds, gathering up his weed off the coffin coffee table and finishing off his beer.

I stood up to leave and Toby asked me where the hell I thought I was going.

"With you guys," I replied.

"Why don't you stay with me?" asked Gloria.

"Yeah dumb-ass, why don't you stay with her," said Toby.

"But I got to work tonight," I protested.

"Two Seconds will cover for you, won't you Two Seconds?"

"Shit man, I don't want to go in. Besides, I owe Ray twenty bucks and I don't want to give it to him."

"Christ, I'll give you the money, just cover for the Squid will ya?"

"I'd appreciate it Two Seconds," I added, fully conscious of what staying might mean.

"Shit, alright. But you owe me Squid."

"Bye," said Toby, waving and smiling, backing out the apartment door.

And then they were gone. Poof, like magic. That's when Gloria straddled me on the couch and pulled off my shirt. That late afternoon I became a man. We fucked like savages. In between bouts of sex we rolled off one another, resting our sweaty bodies side by each, staring up at the ceiling, and telling each other our dreams for the future. I listened to Gloria pant and looked over at her perfect little body thinking, *Now I know true love.* I don't remember falling asleep.

When I woke up, it was dark. Gloria was gone. I could hear the sounds of cars, night noises. I found a note on the kitchen table: *Had to go to work for a few hours Stud, be back at 3. XX OO Gloria.* My heart soared—Stud. I went and drank water from the kitchen tap, then found a beer in fridge. I turned on one of the multiple TVs and watched *Frankenstein* and *The Bride of*

Frankenstein back to back. When it was over, Gloria came back and we fucked until the sun came up. Then we fell asleep.

......

A few weeks later I was back in Lucifer's Tavern with Toby and Two Seconds. We were drinking draft and talking about going places. There were two older men at a table nearby—sleazy, open shirts, gold chains, hairy forearms. They were flipping through magazines and laughing.

"Hey," said one of the men, whose wisps of greasy white hair were pulled tight into a small ponytail, which hung off the back of his balding freckled head like a piece of plump spaghetti.

We all looked over at their table.

"Wanna see my sister?" asked the man, holding up a close-up shot of a shaved beaver; lips spread wide by long, red fingernails. The man and his partner, who was wearing a blue and yellow Hawaiian print shirt, roared with laughter.

"Take a look," he said, tossing the magazine over to our table. It landed spinning open to a sultry looking blonde drooling over a swollen member.

"Christ, lookie here," said Toby grabbing at the nudie mag.

"Let me see," said Two Seconds, snatching the other corner.

The sound of tearing paper followed and I thought to myself, just fucking great. Two Seconds ended up with just the cover page of *Slut* magazine.

The two men looked over.

"You're gonna have to buy that now. That issue is a collector's item," said the man in the Hawaiian shirt.

We all looked at each other for thoughts on how to respond. These guys looked mean and nasty.

"Bullfuckingshit," muttered Toby under his breath as he flipped through the coverless rag.

Ned and Larry were two tables down doing their own magazine reading. Lucifer's looked like the waiting room of a twisted doctor's office.

"Hey, I'm serious," said the man in the Hawaiian shirt. "Yous are gonna have to pay for that. That's ten bucks there. My sister don't come cheap."

The men both roared with laughter. Lydia, who was sitting in her usual corner smacking her gums, laughed along with them, though I don't think she knew why.

I snatched away the magazine from Toby.

"Hey, whatcha doing?" protested Toby.

"Gimme that," I said, ripping the cover away from Two Seconds.

I got up and walked over to the men's table and placed the magazine on top of a small stack of others.

The man with the ponytail glared at me. His skin held a sweaty sheen, and he smelled of Old Spice and alcohol. "You rip it, you own it," he said.

I put my hand on the back of his chair and leaned in close.

"Hey look," I whispered. "We don't want any trouble, and I don't think you do either. We don't want the magazine. Underage kids and pornography: it's not good for you, and it's not good for us. So, why don't I buy you guys a drink and we'll call it square?"

"What, you don't like my sister?" the man with the ponytail demanded in a loud voice.

"How about your father?" retorted Toby from our table.

"What?" asked the man twisting in his chair.

"I said, what about your father?" asked Toby again.

It was like somebody shot our David Crosby look-a-like with gamma rays, like the Hulk. The man pushed back from his table, stood up, came over to our table, clutched Toby's chair by the armrest and spun it around. He grabbed Toby by the front of his shirt, balling it into his fist. Nobody moved. Ned and Larry looked up from their reading and watched nervously. Lydia looked over, opened and closed her mouth a few times, then looked away, as if nothing out of the norm was happening.

"What did you say you little piss turd?!" demanded the man.

"Look, I'm sorry," said Toby, leaning back as far as the chair and the collar of his pulled shirt would allow him.

"Nobody talks bad about the ol' man!"

"Take it easy Lester," said the man in the Hawaiian shirt.

One of the Mommas came rushing over to the brute holding Toby's shirt.

"Hey, we can have none of this. Now please, you sit back down and Momma brings you a drink, on the house," she pleaded.

But the man would have none of it. He kept staring at Toby. Lester was a big man, and he teetered drunk, swaying like a tree in a strong wind. He held onto Toby's Jimi Hendrix tie-dye for both balance and intimidation. Lester balled up his other hand into a fist and held it against Toby's cheek, pushing his knuckles into the flesh a little.

"Look, hey, I'm really sorry," repeated Toby.

I could see the terror in Toby's eyes.

"Hey, hey, you leave dese boys alone now," said Momma, grabbing Lester's arm.

"Get your fucking hands off me bitch," Lester replied, keeping his eyes on Toby.

Marcus, the son of one of the Mommas who ran the bar, heard this and came around. He wasn't a huge guy by any means, but he looked like he was in good shape.

"Okay, you, get out!" yelled Marcus. "Momma, you go call the police."

"Fucking Leb!" hollered Lester, releasing Toby.

Momma began to shoo us out, saying that the cops were on their way and we had to go.

Toby, Two Seconds and I all grabbed our beers and chugged them down in drinking competition style, then boogied out, lickity-split, just as Lester was taking a swing at Marcus, who had backed up near the bar.

We got outside.

"Fucker fucked up my shirt," said Toby, trying with a shaky hand to smooth out Hendrix's scrunched-up face.

"Those guys were a couple of pricks," I noted.

"What do you guys wanna do now?" asked Two Seconds.

"Let's go smoke a fatty," said Toby.

It was Toby's solution to any situation that held any emotional magnitude: smoke a joint.

"I'm gonna bail guys, I'm going to see if Gloria's home," I said.

"I bet you are," said Two Seconds grinning. "I bet you are."

......

When I got to Cockroach Heights, an old lady was coming out, so I grabbed the door and went up without buzzing first. I heard the organ notes of the Doors coming from Gloria's apartment. I knocked. Nothing. I knocked again. The music got turned down. I knocked again and yelled that it was me.

The door opened. There before me was a tall man wearing only jeans and cowboy boots. He had a Harley-Davidson logo tattooed on his bare chest, long wavy hair down to his shoulders, and a moustache that extended down to his chin. He was a real *man*, and he made me very aware of my own underdeveloped, skinny, adolescent body.

"Whaddya want?"

"Is Gloria here?"

"Who are you?"

"I'm her boyfriend, who are you?"

He smirked. He held onto the top of the door and leaned back into the apartment. I could smell his armpits.

"There is a kid here with a greasy Elvis do that claims he's your boyfriend," he said to Gloria, who I could now see was flaked out on the couch like a rag doll. She had a black belt around her left bicep.

"Gloria, whatcha doing?" I asked as I took a step forward into the apartment.

The big biker's palm stopped me.

"Where do you think you're going?"

"Hey, get the fuck off of me. Gloria, who is this asshole?"

"Who is it?" moaned Gloria.

44

"You're not coming in here," he said as he gave me a shove backwards.

"Gloria! It's me, Squid."

"Squid?" Gloria sounded far away.

"Tell this bozo to let me in!"

"Squid, what kind of stupid name is that?" laughed the biker.

"Squid, go away. I don't want you here," she croaked from the couch, waving me away. I couldn't tell if her eyes were open at all.

"Let me in pal."

"She doesn't want to see you, Squidy, so buzz off." As he started to close the door I jammed my foot in the way. He gave me a much harder shove this time and I fell backwards into the hallway and landed on my ass.

I got up and pounded the door with the back of my fist. "Gloria, open up! It's me, Squid! Gloria!" I kept pounding and hollering away. I heard arguing.

Finally the door opened again. It was Gloria. She looked awful. "Squid, go away will ya, I don't want you here."

"What are you doing with this guy? What are you doing. . ."

"Go away Squid!" she screamed.

The door opened wider and buddy reappeared. "You heard the lady, buzz off."

"Fuck you!"

Wham. He sucker-punched me in the nose. I fell backwards again, clutching at my face. I knew he had broken it, the fucker.

"Jesus Christ Larry! Sorry Squid, but you have got to go away. I don't want to see you here again."

And then she just shut the door. I was blown away.

I sat there in the hallway for a while and bled and cried a little. When I heard the music turn back up, I decided it was time to go.

I went to McDonald's and used the washroom to clean up some of the blood. Then I went to the Paranoid Parking Lot and found Two Seconds and Toby having a spitting contest.

"Shit man, what the fuck happened to you?" asked Toby as he arched back and let a gob of spit fly.

"Big asshole named Jesus Christ Larry broke my nose. Got any salad left?"

"I always got salad," said Two Seconds pulling his dope from his pants.

"Jesus Christ Larry? Come on man, tell us what happened!"

So I told 'em. Then we got good and high and laughed and laughed and laughed.

I didn't bother trying to see Gloria again. She had my phone number, knew where I worked. Nothing. I never saw her again, nor Jesus Christ Larry, for that matter.

......

The last time I was in Lucifer's was in the winter of that same year, just after Christmas. Two Seconds and I were in there, and some drunk woman was on the payphone screaming at her boyfriend that he was an SOB and that she didn't give a rat's ass what he did with the goddamn microwave. This woman's rant, combined with the pathetic three-foot plastic Christmas tree, decked out in multicoloured lights blinking on and off in slow motion, created a holiday atmosphere that you could only find at Lucifer's. Charming.

Two weeks after this, Lucifer's Tavern burned down. They

had a suspicious kitchen fire that everybody in their right mind knew was arson. When I heard this I had a vision of Momma and Momma running around in matching negligees and black balaclavas, dousing the place with cans of gasoline.

Shortly after this, maybe a week or so later, we had an ice storm. It was a doozy. Everything ended up coated in three-quarters of an inch of ice. The city looked like Superman's castle.

I was walking—more like sliding—home in the early morning light of dawn, after a party, when I saw the ambulance. It was parked on Bank Street about a block away from the boarded-up windows of Lucifer's. On the sidewalk stood two paramedics staring down at a black mound underneath the ice. I realized the black mound was a person, obviously dead. Then as I got closer I could make out the beard, the nose, and open eyes.

It was Ned. Poor bastard had died right where he normally panhandled. I thought about the people who must have stepped over him, trying to get out of the storm to get somewhere warm and safe. Not a single person had stopped to check to see if ol' Neddy was okay. He'd just lain there, probably drunk, and had gotten covered by the ice.

I was sickened by this, the thought of Ned dying a slow cold death, and nobody helping him. But as I walked home that morning, I smiled at something ol' Neddy would say when he was sitting there in the bar getting loaded: "If there's a hell, well I've got at least two seats reserved!"

AUTOGRAPH

There are drugs to decrease the activity of neurotransmitters in the brain and there are drugs to increase them. Some get you drooling like a starving man in slow motion, while others dry you out and give your stomach knots like you just ate a textbook full of math equations. It's the job of the psychiatrist to keep the chemical soup of the human mind tasting good. The two men smoking by the front door of the Wilford building look like they are in need of some dopamine bouillon. Dad's in the Wilford building. It's an old three-storey brick building filled with pills, drooling and madness. The men watch me as I approach, their eyes follow me like I am a character in a play.

"Hello," I say as I reach for the door handle.

"They'll try and poison you in there," says the one man, wearing a T-shirt with an Andy Warhol print of a Campbell's soup can on it.

"I know it, that's why I stay away from the soup," I tell him, pointing at his shirt as I enter the building.

The elevator is huge, big enough to hold a stretcher and it's slow like a Valium junkie. Whenever you're in it, it's like being in your own private cell. Finally after its mouth opens and spits me out like cheeked meds, there's Dad standing at the adjacent nursing station, scribbling away with the intensity of an accountant in his notebook. He looks up to see who it is and takes a step back in such an exaggerated expression of shock that I don't know whether it's playful or real.

"Jonathan, I'm glad you have come. I've just finished decoding the universe," he tells me with the eureka expression of a world-class physicist.

"Is that so?"

"Oh yes. Come here and take a look," he says, pointing to the calculations in his notebook. "One is God, two is the Son, three is the Holy Ghost, four is the Beatles, five is the Pentagon, six is. . ."

"Listen Dad, I've got some news for you," I tell him, trying to interrupt his incessant chatter.

"Six is your mother because her birthday is on the sixth, seven is a lucky number, eight is Laura because her birthday is on the eighth. . ."

Dad keeps going, telling me the symbolic significance of all numbers up to twenty-six and each letter of the alphabet and how they all correspond. I get lost in Dad's words, just nod my head and say, "Uh huh" over and over. I stare at the rope-burn scabs that have formed on Dad's neck. I imagine his face purple and bulging, trying to grasp for air. Luckily the old beams in the attic cannot hold much weight. I look back to the notebook of scribblings and see Dad's fingers: the index and middle fingers of both hands look like dark brown leather where he holds his cigarettes. The nicotine stains sunset near the knuckles, turning to orange then fading into honey yellow. Dad is now talking about aliens and time travel. Do they give you a handbook when you go crazy? Twelve easy steps to being committed. Craziness for Dummies. Why do they all talk about the same crazy shit?

"Time travel eh?"

"That's right Johnny, while I've been decoding the universe I've discovered that I can time travel. So far I've only been able to go a few hours into the future or the past, but I know with practice that I can go back and save your mother. I'll travel forward, get the cure for cancer and bring it back. You don't have to worry Johnny. Did you bring the cigarettes?"

I hold up the plastic bag like a dead chicken so Dad can see the small rectangular shape of the Export A "green death" carton poking through.

"Excellent, let's go smoke."

Susan, the station nurse, sees the bag and checks it for shaving razors. "Always got to check to be safe," she says, throwing me a big smile.

Dad and I pass Drooling Dan doing his slow hallway shuffle in his dilapidated Valium-blue slippers and grey tracksuit, staring at us like a zombie. We are on our way to what I call "The Chamber." I figure this is the closest approximation to a real gas chamber as I will ever get: a ten-by-ten six-person smoking theatre with the only ventilation being a small window with a tight mesh screen the size of a toaster. My eyes start to water within five minutes. We sit in mismatched armchairs around a beat-up coffee table with a couple of heaping tinfoil ashtrays and some Styrofoam coffee cups. A little radio belts out a tinny version of "Everybody's Got Something to Hide Except Me and My Monkey." Dad nudges me and says, "The Beatles, number four in the universe," then laughs like he's told some sort of really funny joke.

There are two other people in The Chamber, a woman who looks to be in her mid-thirties wearing a pink track suit, and an older man in jeans and a T-shirt with a monster-truck Budweiser logo. Dad's laughter causes the woman in pink to laugh.

"She's a swift one I tell you," says the old guy, motioning at the pink woman with his thumb.

"I'm Bob," he says, extending his other hand.

"This is my son Jonathan," Dad says.

I grab Bob's hand and notice the nicotine stains on his fingers, the familiar tattoo of mental illness. "Nice to meet you," I respond. Bob's hand is clammy and weak.

"Your father is a good man. He and I are the only ones in here who aren't nuts, you know."

"Oh yeah."

"Hey I'm serious," says Bob leaning forward, scrunching his brow. "Your old man and I know about the aliens. And the crazy doctors here don't believe a word we tell 'em. I've been abducted twenty eight times you know. I seen 'em come right down and grab a deer once. They're planning to colonize the earth. They've already taken over the government. That's why they locked me in here. They know I know the truth about what's going on. They put a device in my head to read my thoughts. I tried to drill it out."

With mixed feelings of horror and fascination, I notice the circular patch of hair missing from the right side of Bob's head, just above the ear. I point to the same area on my own head and ask, "Is that from the drill?"

"Yeah, I passed out before I could get the device out, but I think I might have damaged it. I don't think they can read my thoughts all of the time. I do mental experiments eh, and I know they can't read all my thoughts now."

Suddenly the woman in pink starts to laugh real loud. "It's all in his head," she says, saliva flying from her cave of a mouth, gooey saliva connecting upper and lower yellow teeth. She is barely able to get the words out between laughter. Hardly breathing, her head turns an awful shade of red.

"Shut up Doris!" yells Bob.

This causes Doris to laugh even harder. If Doris lost forty pounds and grew out her hair, she wouldn't be bad-looking. Dad leans over toward me, two inches of ash precariously dangling off his cigarette. "She is crazy," Dad says.

"You should ash that smoke."

We sit in The Chamber until Dad has finished three cigarettes and I tell him I cannot take the smoke any longer. I say goodbye to Doris and Bob and now Dad and I are shuffling back down the hall toward his shared room. We pass Drooling Dan again on his endless nomad journey of the hallway. They have put out the little metal snack cart near the day room. Dad grabs a Styrofoam cup. He takes his black pen monogrammed with gold initials from his shirt pocket. How quickly and how far we can fall out of society's good graces. One day you're one of the city's top-paid urban planners and three years later you have lost everything, except for your monogrammed pen.

"What's the date?" asks Dad.

"It's the twenty-eighth, why?" I ask.

"For historical records. Historians will need to have detailed records when they will try to piece together the timeline of my life. It gets especially convoluted with time travel." Dad writes down the date, then consults his ten-dollar plastic watch and notes the time, which he also writes on the lip of the Styrofoam cup. Then he autographs it along the body. "There, one day that cup will be worth millions," says Dad, holding it up as if it were the Holy Grail.

He pours coffee into it and adds a little milk. "Coffee?" he asks.

"No thanks."

He grabs a piece of toast and spreads peanut butter on it, then takes a big bite. "Toast?" he asks while he's chewing.

"No thanks."

"Are you sure? No coffee, no toast?"

"No really Dad, I'm fine."

Drooling Dan passes by. Dad and I follow, moving back down the hall toward his room. I glance in the doorway of the day room and notice Multiple Mike staring like the undead at the TV, his right leg moving up and down like a piston. Tremors. A lot of anti-psychotic drugs cause the muscles to tighten up, the back to stiffen, and they can give you tremors—involuntary ticks and twitches. Some people are never able to stop moving. I wonder if that's true if you are more than one person. According to Dad, Multiple Mike has fourteen different personalities and he is one of only a few patients in the country with this type of disorder. I didn't understand how Dad could know this, but if you're here long enough I guess you find out things.

We enter Dad's room, his bed is the last in a row of three. The beds are separated by movable drapes like a normal hospital. At the end of each bed there's a small corresponding wall unit comprised of a closet and desk and some shelves that are all covered in plastic simulated wood. I sit on the edge of his bed and stare at what looks like fifty used Styrofoam cups on Dad's desk, each with the time and date noted on the lip.

"They're going to have to build a few more airports," says Dad.

"Pardon?"

"Airports for all the people."

"What people?"

"For all the tourists, Jonathan, the tourists." Dad looks at me like I'm daft. "Don't you see? This is going to be a religious holy site. Millions of people will want to come here and visit the homes that we lived in and where I was held prisoner here in this hospital."

"And why would this be?"

Dad leans forward and lowers his voice, his tone becoming serious.

"Jonathan, I'm the chosen one. I'm the second son of God. I will time travel to the future and bring back the cure for cancer, and then I'll go on to colonize other planets to protect the world from overpopulation, and there will be world peace. Each one of those coffee cups will sell for a million dollars because they will become historically important religious icons. When this project takes off it's going to be big. It's going to change the world."

"Okay" I say, trying to sound like I'm convinced what he has said is true.

"Hey, take a cup with you, you never know when you could use a million dollars."

......

I come out and see Dad often, but it's always hard. I look at him talking about aliens and time travel, and he looks so small and sad and crazy. I give him a hug and realize that he stinks like smoke and BO and I just keep hugging him anyway. Then our embrace ends and he looks at me and laughs. "You know it's going to be grand when I get out of here, eh?"

"I know Dad, it's all going to be good."

The nurse sees me and pushes the button behind the counter of the nursing station to bring the elevator up. I get in and Dad remains there—he doesn't have grounds privileges yet, so he can't walk me out of the building. Maybe next week.

He smiles and waves and I smile and wave back, right to the bitter end of the door closing, both of us waving like madmen (he's definitely waving like a madman), me pressed up against the side of the elevator wall, still waving through the rapidly narrowing slit of light and space which is my Dad and his hand waving goodbye. *Sluump*—the elevator door closes; ending our childhood game that we continue to perform on occasions of departure. Dad always waves until he's just a speck. Whether it is him leaving, me leaving, or both of us leaving in opposite directions, we always wave something fierce. It's sort of our way of slowing down time and making that moment last forever, never really leaving each other, just an eternal wave goodbye.

Two months later I get the call from Joey, one of the guys from the rooming house. He found Dad and the three bottles of empty pills. I go over and ID the body. There is blood all over the bed where he bled from the anus. I collect a few of his personal possessions, his notebook and his monogrammed pen. I look at the stack of autographed Styrofoam cups that he kept on top of his dresser. I smile. I grab a cup and throw it in the plastic grocery bag along with all of Dad's stuff. When famous people die their autographs go up in value.

"You never know when you could use a million dollars," I say to the police officer watching me. "You never know."

BEAUTIFUL BRUISES

My love affair with the mud was borne from Lulu, one of the several girlfriends Father had after my parents divorced—as opposed to the ones he had while they were married. Lulu was a hairdresser/beautician with enormous boobs and a big juicy ass that was usually shoved into tight pink pants. She had crazy hair right out of a movie; '50s honey-yellow bee-hive hair. Lulu was almost a stereotype walking around in four-inch heels, smacking her gum loudly and smoking these long movie-star cigarettes in a fancy black holder. But Lulu was no dummy, and with good sense she soon left my alcoholic father. She was attending college part time to become a horticulturist. She loved plants and was always in the garden in the evenings.

"What the hell's wrong with goddamn hairdressing?" Father would ask.

"Nothing Henry, I guess that I prefer plants to people is all."

"What a load of shit. You would die if you didn't have those little old gals to talk to and turn their hair blue."

"Whatever Henry, I'm still going to school," she would insist.

......

Father was always giving her shit about the plants, and always demanding massages. One night while Lulu was at college, Father got real loaded up, went out to the backyard and kicked the shit out of these beautiful giant peony flowers that Lulu just loved. There was nothing left but petals and broken green stems. And if that wasn't enough, Father pulled his pants down right there in the backyard and took a shit on a patch of daisies. He laughed like hell.

The next day when Lulu saw what he had done, she packed her bags and left.

"Goodbye Charley, I can't stay here anymore. Keep your nose clean," she said as she gave my hair a rub.

"Bye Lulu," I said and just watched that great ass swish back and forth down the front lane and into an awaiting cab.

I was fourteen and I loved Lulu. I was heartbroken—but I still had the mud.

......

Two weeks prior to Lulu's sudden departure, she had looked at me and said, "Gee whiz Charley, I think you're really into puberty now. When's the last time you washed your face?"

"What?"

"Charley, come here and show me your face."

I complied and she cupped my chin with those red fingernails and looked at me like she was going to paint my portrait.

"Charley, you've got a lot of blackheads on that nose of yours, it's high time that we clean you up."

Thus began my afternoon of exfoliation.

......

The first thing Lulu did was make me wash my face with soap and hot water. She gave me a tough facecloth that felt like steel wool. "Work the nose, scrub it good," she said hovering over me in the bathroom.

When that was done she sat me at the dining room table and placed a large bowl of steaming milky liquid, with little red rose petals floating in it, in front of me. It smelled of honey and lemon and roses, a wonderful smell, a Lulu smell.

"It's time to open up those pores of yours," ordered Lulu. "Put your head over the bowl and cover yourself with this." She threw me a large white fluffy towel.

I don't know how long my face was in there—ten or twenty minutes, maybe? Time seemed to have stopped. I zoned out. I was in a warm happy place. I was sure this is what it would be like to be in Lulu's bosom.

Then all of sudden Lulu whipped off the towel and brought me back to reality, and then to the couch, where I was told to lay down. She put a steaming hot cloth on my face and told me to relax. I felt my face flush.

The next thing I knew the cloth was off and I was directed back to the chair. Lulu came at me with a metal probe like a demented plastic surgeon in a B-horror film. I was worried, but Lulu's calming voice repeated *Relax*—and so I did.

For twenty minutes Lulu squeezed and poked and worked away at my pores, forcing out the dirt and oils lodged into my adolescent face. When she was done, she looked at me like she had just put the finishing touches on a masterpiece.

"Now for the mud," said Lulu.

"Mud? You just washed my face, why would you put mud on it?"

This made Lulu laugh and pinch my check and tell me that I was a doll face.

"A mud-*mask* silly, a mud-*mask*."

This didn't clarify anything for me at the time, but I just went with what Lulu said.

"This will start to harden and it will start to feel weird. It may sting a little, but that's normal." She spread the runny mud-mask mud, which felt more like paint than mud, all over my face except around the eyes. She brought me back to the couch and told me to lay back down.

With a magician's touch, two giant slices of cucumber appeared. "Close your eyes Charley, and I'll put the cucumber slices on."

"What for?"

"They'll keep you from getting wrinkles."

"What will carrots do?"

"I don't know. I've never tried carrots."

I felt the mud tighten and my face stung with a good kind of pain. After another twenty minutes had elapsed, Lulu removed the cucumbers from my face and ordered me to wash up. When I finally got the mud off and dried my face, my skin felt reborn. It looked healthy, I looked healthy. Lulu looked at me.

"Much better," she said, like it was a very casual thing, as if she'd just straightened a crooked picture.

Then Father came home. He was full of nastiness and liquor. As it was Saturday, Father had been drinking since ten a.m. at the bus station. They started serving early there. "What the *hell* have you two idiots been doing?!" Father slurred.

"Lulu cleaned my face," I replied.

"Lulu did *what?*" he screamed.

"She cleaned my face," I said backing up as Father stumbled toward me.

"Oh yeah, you little shit, I'll clean your face!"

That's when Father belted me on the cheek with a big meaty right hook. I fell down and my eyes welled up. He had beat me before, but I wasn't going to give him any tears. And I didn't. Not even at his funeral. Not a drop.

I picked myself up and faced him. I felt bad for Lulu. She had had her afternoon's work ruined in just one quick punch. I could feel that it was going to be a big black and blue nasty sucker. So much for nice skin. Father raised his hand to strike me again. I flinched a little, but didn't move, didn't shed any tears. He teeter-tottered with that drunken sway, like a tall tree in a strong wind. "You're nothing!" he yelled as little bits of spit flew into my face.

"Fuck you Henry! Don't you hit Charley!" screamed Lulu as she came running out of nowhere, brandishing a wooden rolling pin like a sword.

Father turned to see Lulu coming at him and grabbed her arm. "You fucking bitch! You think you can sit on my son's face?!"

Lulu dropped the rolling pin. Father managed to slap her a few times while he continued to scream obscenities at her.

"You're just an asshole Henry!" Lulu yelled back as she managed to break free of Father's grip.

Father came at her again. I was frozen with fear and didn't know what to do. It wasn't until years later, when I was eighteen, that I finally pushed Father down to the ground. He never tried to hit me after that.

Father had Lulu again and threw her to the ground. She broke the heel of her right shoe on the way down. She had fallen beside the cheap little wooden coffee table with the large green ceramic ashtray on it. Father grabbed the ashtray and threw it against the wall. It shattered into little pieces.

"You fucking bitch! All you do is fuck with those goddamn flowers and my faggot son's face!!!"

It looked like he was going to smash Lulu with his sledgehammer fist, like an ape, but at the last second he hit the coffee table instead. It broke in two. Had it not been made from such cheap material, Father would have broken his hand. Too bad.

Then Father backed up a little, removed his belt. "I'm gonna teach you something reeeeal gooood baby," said Father in a devil's voice.

Lulu's hair had become tangled. It flew out in every direction as if it were the sun. She looked like a wounded animal kicking away at the air with her broken shoe. "Fuck you Henry!" she repeated.

He moved toward her, twirling his belt in the air like a lasso. "You need a good hog-whipping baby, and daddy is gonna give it to ya. Oooyyeaahh!!" he yelled with a big smile.

He stepped back to give himself some room to whip Lulu. He stepped back onto the rolling pin. It was something out of a cartoon. He went flying up into the air and landed with a mighty thud on his back. He was out cold and he started to snore. It was all very anticlimactic. Lulu threw me a big grin with her smudged make-up face and then started to laugh.

"That was damn lucky baby," she said laughing, although there were tears of fear still running down her face.

I just nodded dumbfounded.

. . . . . .

Lulu put some ice on my face and afterwards took me out for a giant sundae at this great restaurant called Benny's. They put Smarties on their sundaes there. I loved that.

"You're going to have one beautiful bruise there, Charley," Lulu said as she sucked at her menthol cigarette.

"Give me a bit of character, eh?"

"Yeah baby," said Lulu as she turned her head and looked out the window, like she was distracted by a car or person walking by. I shovelled mint chocolate chip ice cream down my throat.

Lulu finished her smoke and mashed the butt out in the ashtray.

"Charley," she began, leaning forward over the table.

"Yeah?"

"I don't know how much longer I can stay."

My heart sank. But I didn't blink.

"You should go. I'll be just fine. Don't worry about me," I said as convincingly as possible.

I talked a tough line when Father wasn't beating me or anyone else. The truth was I was scared shitless that Lulu would leave and it would be just Henry and me again. Mom had died shortly after the divorce. She overdosed on antidepressants.

Anyway, I told Lulu not to worry her pretty little head about me. She laughed and told me that I was a sweet kid.

The next day Father had no idea what he had done and asked me if I had gotten into a fight at school. I told him it was summer and there was no school. I told him I fell down. Had I told him he hit me, he wouldn't have believed it, and would have punished me for telling lies. It was a lose-lose situation. Lulu put up with it for two more weeks and then split after the plant incident in the backyard.

......

When I finally did leave, I was eighteen. I finished tying my running shoes, grabbed my suitcase, and spit on the living room carpet. Father threw a beer bottle at my head. It missed and smashed on the wall beside me as I went out the front door.

THE DEAL

The red heart-shaped LED display of the Lifestep 9500 greeted Michael Roberts as he stepped on the exercise machine at 7:01 a.m.

Michael had made a deal with God: burn seven hundred calories in thirty minutes and God would save his brother's life. It was simple. Ride that mean bastard like a mechanical bull, and Danny would be in the clear. Even though Michael, at the age of thirty-nine, was in the best shape of his life, he knew this was going to be a tough one.

Danny had been diagnosed with testicular cancer five years ago and had one of his testicles removed and replaced with a rubber prosthetic. After Danny recovered, he would joke around with his brother, claiming that the testicle was bionic while grinding his pelvis in slow-motion and making the accompanying *Six Million Dollar Man* sound effects.

"Not even Lee Majors had a bionic ball," Danny would say with a big grin so full of life that Michael thought nothing could stop it, not even God.

But last year the cancer had come back and spread into Danny's intestines and stomach. Two operations and three rounds of chemotherapy later, his condition had only worsened. In the last month, his lymphatic system had started shutting down and he was retaining fluid in his legs, feet and scrotum. Danny used to weigh a healthy 190 pounds, then he plunged to a scrawny 140. In the last two weeks, water retention had sky-rocketed him up to 240. His scrotum had become so enlarged that the taut skin was seeping. Even his feet were seeping. If and when Danny did manage to stand up, on extremely long and painful trips to the washroom, he would end up standing in a small puddle of his own fluid. His back and legs were covered in bedsores, and he was emitting an odour of rotting meat. Dr. Adams had told Michael that there was nothing else they could do, it was now in God's hands. That's when the deal came to Michael, that's when he knew it was right.

Michael crossed himself head to heart, shoulder to shoulder, and hit the *start* button.

The contract was signed.

......

The first time Michael made a deal with God he was eight years old. He was with his parents and his little brother at their cottage on Muldrew Lake, in the Muskokas. He had been out walking in the woods with his father and their dog, Doogle. The dog had run ahead on the trail barking after something, and soon Doogle's bark seemed very far away. The sky blackened with an impending thunderstorm.

"Dooooooo-gguule," his father called. "Dooooooo-gguule. Come here boy. Dooooooo-gguuuuule, come here boy."

The wind was picking up, and the rustling of the trees was drowning out both the dog and Michael's father. Finally Doogle's bark, if he was barking, was no longer audible.

Michael and his father felt the first drops.

"We have to head back little man, before we get caught in something really nasty."

"What about Doogle?" asked Michael, in a Walt Disney voice heartbreaking to his father's ears.

"Doogle will be just fine little man. He'll find his own way back, okay buddy? But right now we've got to hurry back before this storm gets really bad and your mom starts to worry about us."

Michael, with sad lips and watery eyes, just nodded in agreement. They headed back down the trail. Three quarters of the way home, it started coming down hard. Witchy cackles of lightning and thunder were upon them, and Michael's father was not only worried about Doogle, but also about themselves and Karen and Danny back at the cottage. And that's when Michael experienced the *crack*. It was beyond sound and brighter than light itself. A tree was struck by lightning only fifty metres from where they had just been, and the floor of the forest danced and slithered with the blue and white dissipating electrical light.

The tree started to fall and Michael started to cry. His father grabbed him fireman-style over his shoulder and ran like the devil was upon him. Michael hung on to his father's shirt like the good guy he had seen on TV holding onto the hood of the high-speed car. Michael could hear the crescendo of splitting wood and knew it would be only seconds before they got hit. Michael never really worried though; he knew his father would take him out of harm's way. He had seen his father play football, and he had heard all the tales of university glory—tales of being the best quarterback who ran the most yards in the least amount of time. Michael began to low-pitch hum as he bounced on his father's back, producing what he thought would be the sound North American Indians made as they danced around a fire.

Michael wasn't sure if it was a leaf or the wind, but something brushed his cheek just before the incredible earth-shaking BOOM of the tree smashing the ground. But that was all. No pain, no flesh being ripped or cut, no broken bones. Just the sound of his father's heavy breathing and the rain coming down hard.

They ran like this for twenty minutes, Michael occasionally doing his Indian hum as he continued to bounce upside down on his father's back until they safely arrived back at the cottage—safely back without Doogle.

The next morning Michael awoke without Doogle's familiar lapping against his face. He smelled bacon and coffee and heard his father chopping wood outside.

"Hi baby, how about some bacon and eggs?" asked his mother when he appeared in the kitchen doorway wearing his Scooby Doo pyjamas.

"Where is Doogle?" asked Michael, knowing in his heart that the dog was lost, maybe forever.

His mother squatted down so they were eye to eye and placed her hands on his shoulders. "Doogle might not come back honey. A bear or a raccoon might have gotten him."

Michael didn't say anything. He thought about what his mother had told him when Sam his goldfish died: Sam had gone to goldfish heaven. Maybe Doogle had gone to doggie heaven? But God decided who went to heaven and when— Michael knew this. That's when it struck him.

Last week he had been fishing off the end of the dock when he lost his favourite fishing lure, the red and white spoon his grandfather had given to him for a birthday present, known as the "Red Devil," to the rocks of Muldrew Lake's dark underbelly. Wearing his black rubber Canadian Tire snorkelling-mask, Michael had repeatedly tried to rescue the Red Devil from the hellish ear-popping depths below. Michael had given up. The pressure on his ears had been too much. But now he knew if he were able to get the Red Devil, God would bring back Doogle.

After breakfast Michael impatiently waited for his mother's prescribed hour-before-swimming-to-avoid-cramps to pass. Finally after a torturous repetition of "Is it time yet?" Michael's mother let him go in at the fifty-minute mark. As she watched him run down toward the dock with his flippers and mask, she turned to Peter and said, "I thought he would have been more upset about Doogle. All he wants to do is go swimming."

The light shone through the water like a dusty curtain blowing in the window of an old haunted house, illuminating the small iridescent sunfish nibbling at the green and black rocks on the bottom of the lake. Michael watched this strange world through his mask, which held a horizon of rising water. It took some time, but he finally found the glint of the Red Devil trapped deep down amongst the rocks. Michael was nervous about not being able to get the lure, nervous that he wouldn't be able to save Doogle.

After his sixth attempt Michael was getting tired. He had swallowed a good portion of Muldrew Lake. He had been in the water for an hour and his lips were blue, and his fingers and toes had turned to prunes. No lure, no Doogle, thought

Michael. His mother called to him to get out of the water, he had been in long enough she said. Michael replied that he just wanted to do one last dive. And on that note, Michael pulled the mask down from his forehead, crossed himself head to heart and shoulder to shoulder, took a giant breath of air and dove down toward the lure with the intention of not coming up without it.

When Michael hit that spot, the spot where the pressure was too much, the spot where his ears popped and cracked, the spot where his lungs ached, the spot where he always gave up, he just kept going. He had learned in church that Christ had suffered for him. He knew he had to suffer too. He would suffer and Doogle would be brought back. This was the deal he had made with God.

As he got closer and closer to the lure, the pain in his ears and chest grew worse and worse. He needed air but he just kept on kicking. With a desperate outstretched hand he managed to grasp the Red Devil with his thumb and index finger. He had it. He moved it into his palm and clenched it like a rosary. Then it was back up. Michael was now out of breath. He had just made it past the halfway point to the surface, when he started taking on water.

Michael's father yanked him out of the lake, held him up by his feet to clear his lungs of water, then performed mouth-to-mouth. Michael quickly regained consciousness and promptly puked up a combination of lake water, scrambled eggs and bacon onto his father's soaking wet Levi's. He looked down at his right hand; it was bleeding. The hook of the lure had pierced the flesh of his hand between his thumb and forefinger. Michael looked up at his father who was simultaneously displaying the looks of shock, joy, and anger, like some sort of twisted Picasso. Michael, age eight, smiled and said, "I got the lure Dad!"

After a trip to the hospital and receiving what seemed to be an endless lecture about the dangers of swimming, Michael was put to bed by both his parents with a belly full of his favourite foods—hamburgers and chocolate ice cream. He listened to his little brother cry and his parents hushed words of concern over him, "What if anything had happened?" Michael, his hand snugly bandaged, fell asleep with the lure on his bedside table, next to a picture of himself and the dog.

Michael awoke to familiar barking. He sat up and screamed out, "Doogle!"

Doogle was back—covered in burrs and scratches, mind you, but he was back and Michael was elated. He thanked God for keeping up his end of the deal. He thought of telling his parents about the deal, but he knew they wouldn't believe him.

......

At the fifteen-minute mark the Lifestep 9500 told Michael that he had burned 346 calories. Michael Roberts lagged by four calories. Large parabolas of sweat had formed on the front and back of his T-shirt. His legs burned from lactic acid and his eyes burned from salty sweat.

"Fuck me!" he yelled out. An elderly woman in unflattering spandex and a Mickey Mouse T-shirt threw him a dirty look. Michael thought about the tube sticking out of Danny's stomach and his legs started moving faster almost involuntarily.

Michael had made other deals with God. He had swum fourteen kilometres and almost drowned, but Kate had said yes when he asked for her hand in marriage. Michael had run a marathon to get a job promotion. He became the head of the financial department.

Now he was running for Danny. His legs were moving independently. He had found a rhythm. This was God's rhythm. Michael began to hum. He hummed to the rhythm of the machine, to the rhythm of God. He was down to the last three minutes. He knew he was going to make it. He cried hot tears of joy and pain. He cried for Jesus, he cried for Danny, and he cried for himself. His legs were in terrible pain, but not Danny's pain, and he pushed himself even harder.

Just before the Lifestep 9500 turned off its completed thirty-minute cycle, its LED display flashed 700. His legs slowed down as he felt the machine's sudden lack of resistance. The sounds of the gym rushed back into his ears. He was done. It was confirmed, he had made it. Danny had made it.

He got off the machine, his legs rubbery and sore and his T-shirt completely soaked. He headed for the showers. As the hot water fell on Michael, he thought about the headlines in the paper, "Miracle Recovery, Doctors Unable to Explain." He thought about what Dr. Adams might say to the reporters, how science could not explain this, that this was truly a miracle.

Michael dressed, went outside to his car, and drove straight to the hospital. He needed to see Danny right away.

......

The familiar smell of the cancer ward hit Michael like a child entering a musty attic. The plastic-tube cobwebs of dying were everywhere. Laboured breathing and beeping machines echoed in the halls like a horror movie soundtrack. Relatives and loved ones waited, sleeping in uncomfortable chairs. They waited for recovery, or waited for death. Things on this floor were pretty one-sided.

Michael rounded the corner to Danny's room, expecting to see Kate or his father. But the room was empty. The flowers, the nameplate at the top of the bed, and Danny were gone. Michael spun around and headed to the nurse's desk to ask where they had moved...

Dr. Adams was standing in front of him.

"When?" asked Michael.

"This morning about eight. Your father and Kate have been trying to reach you since then. I told them to go home. They were here for some time. I told them that if you came in I would send you home. I'm so sorry Michael."

Michael shook Dr. Adams' hand and said,

"Thanks. Thanks for all your help."

......

The bar was thick and smooth, accented by dark polished wood and plush carpets. This is where Michael and Danny had come to celebrate Michael's job promotion. Michael now took a seat down from a man who was watching hockey on TV. The bartender came down and asked Michael what he wanted to drink.

"Two double single-malt scotches on the rocks," ordered Michael, holding up two fingers to avoid confusion.

"Any brand?"

"Whatever is fine."

The bartender brought back the drinks and placed them on cork coasters in front of Michael.

"Cheers," said the bartender.

Michael looked at the drinks. He moved them beside one another, close, like family. That's when he noticed it on his right hand. He grabbed the first scotch and took a sip, keeping his eye on the little scar, the memory of a childhood deal.

Michael took out his keys. The old worn fishing spoon, his good luck charm, hung amongst them. He unwound the spoon from the key ring and dropped it into the other glass of scotch. He threw down some money.

All the way to his car, Michael held his breath.

CLOWN FACE

When I came in, the party was going full force. A hundred pieces of winter footwear greeted me in the narrow hall by the front door. I removed my own and attempted unsuccessfully to clear the entrance without my socks absorbing a fantastic quantity of salty boot juice. God I hate that. You know, a pair of clean dry socks is highly underrated. So to get a soaker first thing, it put me in a foul mood straight off.

As I careened down the hall I couldn't see anything but green lasers, smoke and the outlines of scantily clad women. Kevin had gotten this guy DJ Delicious to spin and put on the whole E-raver light show thing. Slow hypnotic Enigma stuff. Great if you were high, as I'm sure ninety percent of the people were, but pretty piss poor if all you wanted to do was get drunk and forget your ex-wife.

It was Kevin's place by the way. Place—ha. Don't want to make it sound too pedestrian. How about a gorgeous loft with cathedral ceilings in the downtown core—and just a ten-minute walk to the university? Kevin came from old money, which allowed him to stay in school and have this ridiculous pad. English undergrad is where we met and became friends. I called it quits after my degree, thought I would follow my dream and become a writer.

Kevin is still in school doing his PhD in animal psychology, designing sex toys for chimpanzees. I shit you not, sex toys for chimps. Apparently they've got all these sexually frustrated chimps locked up at the zoo and they are getting pretty darn squirrelly. That's where Kevin comes in. I haven't seen these toys yet, but I just keep thinking of dildos that look like bananas. Or hairy humpable coconuts.

So I made my way to the kitchen, squeezing past chemically fuelled undergrads—most likely Kevin's students—and found the fridge. Even Kevin's fridge was over the top, like that frigging monolith in *2001: A Space Odyssey*, one of those big silver monsters with the freezer on the bottom, ice machine, you know, the whole shit. I could envision his sexually frustrated chimps pounding away on that thing. So I open the door, it's bank-vault heavy, and *wham* I'm squinting in the tracker-beam light of this science-fiction beast. And guess what? All that was in there were vitamin-infused smart drinks, bottled water and diet ginger ale. Jesus Christ, where was all the fucking beer?

A waif of a girl with black saucer eyes, wearing nothing but skin-tight spandex and a white fuzzy bra, like friggin' Peter Cottontail strapped to her tits, asked me to please pass her an orange neuro-cocktail.

"How old are you?"

"Twenty-one," she said.

"Jesus Christ. Here's your drink."

"Thanks. Do you believe in God?"

"No."

"Oh. You're sexy for an old guy," she said running her naughty tongue across the bottom of her top teeth.

"Fuck, no wonder Kevin never got married."

She swooped in, pressed up against my body, grabbed my left earlobe with her incisors and gave me a little love bite, pulled back and hissed softly, "Fuck, maybe later, if you're a good boy." And like a tab of acid at a Grateful Dead concert, *poof*, she was gone. Back into the fog and lights of the dance floor, which was sort of the whole apartment. I went straight back to the front door, found my boots, and headed for the beer store.

......

I found myself under harsh fluorescent lights in a long line with all the other desperate losers two minutes before close. A beer-store employee stood behind me, his hand on the deadbolt. He watched the clock on the wall, watched as the red needle of the second hand came arcing up toward the *12*, signifying 11 p.m., closing time.

He was just about to turn the deadbolt when a clown came running in. And when I say clown, I'm not talking about some drunk joker looking for a king can of Maximum Ice. No, I mean white face, red nose, pom-pom buttons, rainbow wig—an honest-to-God clown. Except this clown wasn't like that, this clown was sadder, like he had been around the block a few times, like he had seen some hard clown life, taken one too many cream pies to the face. It was a hobo clown. Patchwork, lots of browns and a black bowler hat.

"You just made it," I said as *click*, the beer-store clerk locked the dead bolt.

"That wouldn't have been funny," said the clown with a smile and a female voice.

I looked again, and I could now see that there were female features behind that makeup.

Just then a gruff little man, a hobo type himself, came scooting down the line making his way to the exit, bag of beer clutched tight, when he looked up and saw the clown behind me.

"Good Jesus!" said the man putting his arm on me, eyes wide. "I oughta quit drinking, I'm seeing clowns!" He roared with laughter. Several people in line smiled.

The clown put her hands on her hips and made a silly angry face at the man.

I turned to the clown and asked her, "So, what's a nice clown like you doing in a place like this?"

"Going to get drunk like the rest of you."

"Yeah," I said and I didn't know what else to say, so I turned around and faced forward and waited to order my beer.

The line moved quickly enough. Before I knew it I was ordering, and then I was standing in the beer-store parking lot, holding my twelve-pack, watching a clown walk to her pink and purple polka-dotted VW bug. I don't really know what possessed me, I guess I was feeling lonely or something, but I yelled over to the clown.

"Yeah, what?" she yelled back.

"You got another fifty clowns in that car or what?"

She turned back around and kept walking toward the car.

"No, just me," she replied.

"You want to go to a party?"

She opened the door, put her beer inside, and turned back to me and asked, "What kind of party?"

"It's kind of a rave I guess. An old friend of mine, he is a prof at the university, he's got this big loft apartment and he hired this DJ, DJ Delicious. He's got the whole smoke and lights thing going on. There are a bunch of people there running around on E, dancing, smoking pot. It's not really my kind of scene, but I thought maybe *you* might fit right in."

"Why are you going if it's not your scene, why don't you just go home, or go somewhere else?"

"Like I said, my old friend, Kevin, he has been bugging me to go to this party for weeks and I told him I would go."

"Yeah? I don't know. I don't think so," she said, but she didn't move.

"Come on, all the stoners will love you. I just would like some company to drink my beer with. You know, somebody who's not jacked up on ecstasy or acid or whatever. What do you say?"

I could see that she was thinking about it.

"Do you usually try and pick up clowns?"

"Only when I'm at children's birthday parties or when the circus is in town."

She smiled and asked, "Is it far?"

"Only a few blocks away."

"Okay, but I'm not going to stay long, only for one beer."

"Fantastic."

"Just one."

"Sure."

"Okay, hop in," she said.

And so I did.

When I was in the car, I found myself visually overwhelmed by the dashboard. Every trinket imaginable was glued to it: an Eiffel Tower, a Buddha, a dozen or so clowns, a Statue of Liberty, bottle caps, seashells, R2-D2, a skull, plastic animals, a compass, Homer Simpson, a snow globe, a picture of Elvis, a pair of Bruce Springsteen tickets, an *I Love NY* button, a knight from a chess set, a champagne cork, and lots, lots more.

"Wow! Holy shit, look at all this crap!"

"Yeah, my car is a walking, or should I say driving, scrapbook. It's mostly mementos from places I've travelled to."

"Cool. Very cool. By the way, I'm Trevor," I said extending my hand.

"Natasha," she said, taking my hand. "Pleased to meet you. So, where the hell are we going?"

"Take a left."

......

There was a parking spot right in front of Kevin's building. The smell of pot was strong as we came around the corner to Kevin's front door. You could feel the bass notes rippling from within the apartment. We entered and discarded our footwear on the mountain of boots. I managed to get another soaker from the mountain's salty spring. We squeezed past a young couple who were basically eating each other's tonsils, and moved toward the source of deafening sound.

I was feeling good that Natasha was with me. I mean it was weird and all, moving through the fog and fragmented strobe-lit bodies with a clown in tow, a clown I had just met. But somehow it seemed natural. Maybe natural isn't the word, maybe I should say comfortable. Natasha seemed so easy to talk to, as if we had known each other for years. So now I found myself in a place where I could neither talk nor think.

I was determined to find Kevin, make my appearance known to him so he couldn't bug me later about not showing up, then get the fuck out of there. There seemed to be a hundred people in there all saucer-eyed, gyrating and sweating. Many were dressed like devils for some reason. I thought, Christ, maybe I am truly in hell and I'm never going to find Kevin.

As we made our way through the soupy fog, I spotted a white beacon in the corner of the room. Some might have said an angel, if they were high enough. He looked more like a cross between Tom Wolfe and the Glad garbage-bag guy—it was Kevin. There he was in a white three-piece suit with a matching white shirt, tie and shoes. Girls in devil costumes were draped on Kevin's arms.

"Kevin!" I yelled, waving.

As we approached I looked at the people we were passing. Then it dawned on me that most were dressed in this heaven or hell motif.

"Trevor, where is your costume?" asked Kevin, grabbing my hand and shaking.

"Forgot it was a costume party."

Kevin pouted and shook his head.

"Shame on you. But somebody remembered?" asked Kevin.

"This is Natasha. I have no idea who she is, but she seems to be a bit of a comedian."

Nobody laughed at my joke. Maybe it was too loud in there, or maybe I wasn't that funny.

"Pleased to meet you," said Kevin with a grin that Satan would have been proud to wear, "and these two little devils are Cherry and Blossom."

"Pleased to meet you both. Listen, Kevin, is there a place to go that's not so loud?" I yelled.

"Can I borrow him for just a second?" asked Kevin.

"Sure," Natasha answered.

Kevin pulled me a few feet away.

"Listen man, how long has it been since Cathy, eleven months?"

"It will be a year next week."

"Fuck man, you need to get laid. See those two, they are ready to party. Horny little devils Trevor, horny little devils. Are you hearing me?"

"Yeah. Look, I just want to talk to Natasha over there."

"The clown? You want to fuck the clown?"

"No, I just want to have a beer and talk. What's wrong with you?"

"Listen dude, who is she, is she hot? Cause I can't tell with that outfit she is wearing. Tits can't be that big."

"Jesus Christ, give it a rest will you?"

"Listen Trevor, you want to fuck the clown, it's none of my business, but you need to get laid. This party is for you man, for you to get laid so you can move on with your life. Cathy was a bitch. There are tons of young hot girls here all jacked up and looking for love. Take the devil by the horns and fuck some devil ass. Got it?"

"Got it."

"So who's the clown?"

"I told you, I have no idea, I met her at the beer store and brought her over."

Kevin gave me a look that was somewhere between bewilderment and anger.

"Are you fucking kidding me?"

"No."

"Come on Trevor, you don't even know if the girl is good-looking."

"So?"

"So? Listen dude, hot devils vs. a baggy clown. Are you nuts?"

I guess the look on my face wasn't the happiest either, cause after a small pause of staring each other in the eye, Kevin says, "Okay, go down the hall to my bedroom, furthest door on your left—nice and quiet."

"Thanks."

"Condoms are in the nightstand drawer."

......

I led Natasha down the hall and into Kevin's room. When we shut the door, the music was muted, and suddenly I felt awkward. I didn't know what to say. We looked around. It was a big room with dark green walls. Kevin had spent a few years in Africa studying his chimps, so there were several wooden masks hanging around the room. Perhaps a tad spooky. The room had a balcony with sliding glass doors, a beautiful view of downtown, and a king-size bed with winter coats piled on it like they had jumped on each other after winning the World Series.

"Nice room. Want to have that beer now?"

I was happy Natasha had broken the silence. "Yeah, for sure. Do you want one of mine?"

"Moosehead, eh? Sure. So why did you bring me in here?"

she asked putting her own six-pack of Heineken down on a table near the wall.

"Um, well, I thought we could just talk. You could have your beer. Then I, we, could leave, but not together, just leave. Know what I mean?"

"You nervous all of a sudden?"

"Maybe. Actually not really nervous, just feeling a little awkward maybe. I haven't spoken to anyone, a woman that is, for quite some time." I passed her a beer.

"Thanks," she said, then walked over to the balcony doors and looked out.

I walked over to stand beside her and took a sip of my beer. We both watched the lights of the city. She didn't say anything about what I had just said. She just let it slide and by doing so, made me feel at ease again.

"So what does Kevin do at the university?"

"He is an animal research psychologist—chimps mostly."

"Interesting. What do you do, Trevor?"

"I work at a software company editing computer manuals. That's my day job. I really want to be a writer. I mean, I am a writer, I just can't get anything published."

"You working on a novel or something?"

"Well actually I have a novel, I just can't get it published."

"Hey, good for you. You know, there are tons of people who want to be writers and they never get their shit together enough to actually write something. At least you got it down."

"Yeah, I guess, but an unpublished novel and a novel that's never written, not much difference."

"What? Are you crazy? Of course there is a difference. Better to have tried and failed than to have never tried at all."

"You think?"

"For sure," she said, taking a sip of her beer.

I took a swig myself.

"So, what about you? What's the deal with the clown gig?"

"Well I'm an actor, but acting doesn't pay the bills in this town, so the clown thing is my bread and butter. I also do performance art in the market. Ever see that woman covered head to toe in blue, standing like a statue?"

"Yeah, is that you?"

"Yeah. I do that more for fun. I actually manage to make a few hundred on a good day. I do the occasional play at the GCTC or at the Ottawa Little Theatre, but the clown thing is my main event."

"Main event?"

"Yeah."

Natasha took a sip of her beer. I looked at her makeup. It kind of glistened in the light.

"You want to use the bathroom to wash that stuff off?"

"Why, want to see if I'm good looking?"

I smiled at this and said no.

"Liar."

"No really, I don't care what you look like, I just want to drink my beer. However, if you smelled bad, I would tell you to go and take a shower."

"How about if I just stunk, like showering wouldn't help the situation?"

"Then we wouldn't be having this conversation."

"How about if we were in love, then I developed this..."

"Wait, wait, wait, hold on, in love? I don't even know you."

"Trevor, this is hypothetical, relax. Say you were in love

with somebody, not me, just somebody, and then they developed this disease, this stinky disease where they gave off this really foul odour. I mean really, really stinky."

"Okay, and so?"

"So, let's say you could get an operation so you couldn't smell anymore, which would mean you really couldn't taste much either, would you do it?"

"Would I get the operation?"

"Yeah, so you could be with the woman you loved."

I took a sip of my beer and thought about it.

"Yeah, I guess I would if I really loved her. That would be tough though, giving up your olfactory sense like that. But yeah, I would do it."

"Cool," she said and sipped her beer.

"So, are you going to wash that off or what?"

"Like no. It's a costume party, which you neglected to tell me, so I fit right in. And besides, it's a bitch to get off. I need cold cream and stuff. I'd rather do it at home, it makes such a mess."

"So I'm stuck with this clown am I?"

"Are you going to wash your makeup off?"

"What makeup?"

"Oh, that's your real face is it?"

"Ha ha," I said.

"Yeah, it would be tough giving up your sense of smell, but harder for some than others I think."

"What do you mean?"

"Well there was this guy I used to date, Gordon was his name, and he lived through his nose. He was big into wine and fine food. He was a real cocky son of a bitch, pretentious as all hell. He was always saying, *Smell this* and *Can you smell it, the hint of pine?* or *Can you smell it, the hint of mango?* or some such shit. There was always a hint of something. And he always had to talk about the goddamn food for hours, pontificating on what it tasted like. He could never just eat the stuff and enjoy it. Awful."

"So what happened to Gordon?"

"I snapped one day. It was my birthday. Gordon took me out to this ridiculously expensive restaurant, the kind where the food comes on these really big plates and the food is really small."

"Gotcha."

"Anyway, the sommelier comes over and Gordon goes into this whole production showing off all he knows about wine. The guy brings over four different wines for Gordon to try before he settles on something completely different. So I'm pissed off and I'm starving. So I tell Gordon not to dick around when ordering, that I want to eat. So the waiter comes over and I order the twenty-two-dollar scallops for an appetizer and Gordon orders some warm beet salad. Twenty-two bucks just for my appetizer. Insane. Anyway, it takes forever for the food to come and in the meantime I have to listen to Gordon talk about the wine, what it tastes like. When my scallop appetizer finally does come, there are two scallops. Two. I friggin' lost it at Gordon. Told him he was a pretentious SOB as I stabbed both scallops with my fork, wolfed them down in one big bite and told him we were finished."

"Seriously?"

"You bet. I went straight to Harvey's and got myself a cheeseburger."

"That's really funny."

"Yeah, and oh, you know what I forgot to tell you? You

know what that asshole bought me for my birthday? An electric wine opener. Can you believe that?"

"Nice. Sounds like you two had a lot in common."

"Gimme another beer will ya?"

"Thought you were only staying for one."

"Changed my mind."

......

We kept on chatting like that, laughing, drinking beer. A few people came in to drop off or pick up a coat, but mostly it was quiet, except for those underlying bass notes that penetrated the wall, reverberating throughout the entire apartment, probably the whole building. About an hour or so later the door flew open and this young couple come staggering into the room, a pair of lip-locked flesh beasts. They came over and flopped down on the bed beside the pile of coats. Natasha and I were on the floor, resting our backs on the bed. I guess they didn't notice us, or they did and didn't care, but they started going at it, right then and there. We both turned our heads just in time to see buddy's hand slide into missy's pants.

"Let's go dance," Natasha suggested.

"Sure, let's go."

......

We hit the dance floor, half drunk and full of giddiness. We danced like John Travolta and Uma Thurman. I busted out some retro '80s breakdance moves and had Natasha in stitches. But she topped me with some robot moves and mime stuff that only a true clown could perform.

I hadn't moved like that in years and I was tired and sweaty.

"Beer break?" I suggested.

"Sounds good. Look, I'm hungry, you want to get outta here and get something to eat?"

"Sure. Cheeseburger and poutine?"

"Now you're talking my language. Elgin Street Diner?"

"Sounds good."

When we went back to the room to get our jackets and the rest of the beer, the young couple who had been on the bed had rolled off onto the floor and were full on, buck naked, fucking. All I saw was a skinny white ass bobbing up and down, a blur of hands and hair, and a quick flash of nipple.

Natasha and I looked at each other and laughed.

On the way to the front door, Kevin stopped me.

"Are you going to nail the clown?"

"Jesus man, I don't know, we're just drinking beer."

"Give her this and she'll ride your cock like a gorilla in heat," said Kevin as he slipped a little pink heart-shaped pill into my hand.

"No, it's okay, really."

"Here, take one for yourself, it will do you good."

"Fine, thanks," I said, although I had no intention of taking them.

"Good luck," said Kevin.

I gave him the finger.

As we left the building Natasha said, "What did your friend want?"

"He gave me these pills, I think they're ecstasy."

"Oh yeah. Want to get high?"

"I don't think I do well with drugs. I get all paranoid."

"Cool. Let's eat, then drink more, if you are up for it?"

"I'm game. You okay to drive?"

"Yeah, get in."

......

When the food arrived, Natasha had me talking about my novel.

"Sounds fascinating. I would love to read it."

"Whenever you are having trouble sleeping, this is the book for you."

"I highly doubt it."

"Enough about me. What about you? Why did you become a thespian? And how did you decide to be a clown? Did you wake up one day and say, 'I should be a clown'?"

"Actually, my father was a clown in the Polish circus. He came to Canada and fell in love with my mother and tah-dah, here I am. He told me when I was a little kid that one of the greatest things you can do in life is to make somebody laugh. It's something that has always stuck with me, and it's something I believe. You know, there are so many people out there who are negative and pissed off and just wanting to drag you down with them. It's crazy. And that negativity is infectious, so I kind of see myself as this clown superhero, a kind of balance. The world needs more clowns, more laughter."

"I like that. That's really cool. So where are your parents now?"

Natasha smiled a sad smile, which seemed exaggerated because of her makeup.

"Well that's a bit of a sad story. My mother died in a car accident when I was ten and then my father just fell apart. Started drinking heavily. Pretty soon he was drunk all the time. I came home one day after high school and found him dead in the backyard. He had fallen off the roof while trying to shovel it. Two feet to the left or right and he would have been fine, but he managed to land right on the cement bird feeder. Snapped his neck."

"Sorry," I said. I didn't know what else to say.

"Don't worry about it, that was a long time ago," she said taking a big bite of her burger.

At that moment something happened. I can't really explain it. Suddenly I had all this respect for this person, maybe because she was so open and honest about her life. I don't know, might have been the alcohol too. I felt so relaxed with her, like I could tell her anything and not be judged or anything.

We finished our food and when we got back outside it had started to snow. "Know where we parked?" asked Natasha.

"Yeah."

"Well I live half a block from there. You still up for that drink? Maybe a little whisky and Roxy Music?"

"Whisky and Roxy Music? Wow, yeah, okay, sounds great," I said, and she grabbed my hand and we started to walk. It felt so natural, like eating or sleeping, like something you would just do everyday. Maybe because I'm not hooked into my own emotions all that well, or maybe Cathy had scarred me a little, but normally I think I would have pulled back, would have gotten all weird, would have over analyzed it all. I think I would have normally ended up ruining the moment. But I didn't. I just went with it. My hand in hers, like puzzle pieces connecting.

She lived in a small one-bedroom on the top floor of a three-storey walk-up. When we got to her door she turned and faced me, grabbed me by the shirt collar and pulled me in for a kiss. She tasted of cheeseburgers and beer and I could smell the cream makeup on her face. Spectacular.

After a minute of this she pulled back.

"Sorry, I don't normally go around kissing people I have just met at the beer store," she said.

"Neither do I."

"Liar," she said as she opened the door.

She didn't have a lot of stuff, furniture that is, but her walls were covered head to toe in framed photographs, posters, postcards, record albums, etc.

"Wow, you do have an eye for the eclectic."

"You think? I'm going to change out of this and you'll finally get to see the real me."

"Maybe you should leave the face paint on, unless it's bothering you?"

"Why, you worried that I'm ugly, or are you just kinky?"

"No, nothing like that, it's just that you never really get a chance like this. I mean, everyone is so superficial, they base everything on looks and if you take the make up off, I don't know, it will be like I'm not really finding out who you are. Does that make any sense?"

"Yeah it makes sense. But how about if I told you that I want to show you what I look like right away, before we go any further?"

"Why do you want to do that?"

"Because of the fire. Because of the scars."

She said it in a way that I couldn't tell if she was serious or not.

"Really?"

"What if I answered yes?"

"I don't think I would care either way."

"Tell you what, I'll leave the makeup on for now, I'll just change my clothes."

She put Roxy Music on the stereo, fixed me a drink, and then went into her bedroom to change. When she came back she looked totally different. She was wearing jeans and a tight fitting red shirt. Definitely not the lumpy body of the clown she was before. And now she had shoulder length blonde hair. But she still had the makeup on.

"You look different."

She grabbed her drink and joined me on the couch.

"You like?"

"Me like."

"You still haven't seen the face though."

"True, but it doesn't matter."

"Doesn't it? What if you met someone, fell in love, but then they were horribly scarred in an accident, a fire."

"I would stick around."

"You think? You know, you think you know somebody, then one day they tell you that they can't bear to look at you anymore, that they thought they could adjust to the new look, that with a bit of time they could get used to it, but they couldn't."

"Did that happen to you?"

Natasha didn't say anything, just drained her drink. Then she leaned over and slowly kissed me on the cheek.

"I'm going to wash this off now, okay?"

"Okay," I agreed.

I heard the water going in the bathroom. I sat there on

the couch and waited. I took a sip of my drink and closed my eyes and listened to the music. The water shut off and Natasha come back into the room.

"Here I am," she said.

I opened my eyes.

STAR GAZING

"I got the kid Marlene, and we're not coming back until tomorrow, got it?!" screamed Bobby McLay into the phone.

Stanley and his father were standing in a dilapidated phone booth located beside Dan's Confectionary in the heart of "Star Park—Motorhome and Campground Facility."

Bobby bent down, covering the mouthpiece, and looked Stanley square in the eyes.

"It's your mother, she wants to speak to you. So help me to Christ Stanley, if you tell your mother where we are I'll pack us up and we'll move somewhere else, got it?"

Little Stanley's eyes welled with tears, for he was unable to articulate where he was even if he wanted to. Being six, Stanley was only familiar with a ten-block radius of his own house. He knew the route to school, knew the route to Grandma's house and knew the route to Mac's Milk to buy candy. For the most part, this comprised Stanley's geographic world view. Right now he didn't have a clue where he was.

"Stanley honey?!"

"Hi Mommy."

"Stanley, tell Mommy where you are?"

"I don't know."

"Come on Stanley, you can tell Mommy."

"We're camping, Mom," whispered Stanley.

"Gimme that," said Bobby, snatching the phone away from Stanley. "I'll see you tomorrow, Marlene, I'm gonna spend some time with my son."

He slammed down the receiver.

"Jesus, Stanley! I told you not to tell her where we are."

"I didn't, I just said we were camping."

"Yeah well, you need to listen more. I'm your father you know."

A tear ran down Stanley's cheek.

"Don't worry about it," said Bobby.

"I didn't say, I just said we were camping," muttered Stanley looking down at his muddy sneakers.

"Okay, okay, enough already, let's get some wood and set up the camper."

......

The bell on the door rang. A chubby lady, her hair in pink curlers, sat reading a *People* magazine behind the cashier counter. There was a small black-and-white TV in the corner. Vanna White was turning letters.

"Go find us something to eat son," said Bobby patting Stanley on the back of the head.

Bobby walked up to the counter.

"Hiya," said Bobby.

The woman looked up from her magazine.

"What can I gettcha?"

"I'll take two packs of du Maurier Light King, please."

"Anything else?"

96

Bobby glanced around the counter and grabbed some Hot Rods.

"These too."

The woman noticed the blue, well-endowed hula dancer cavorting with a snake on Bobby's forearm when he grabbed for the sausage sticks.

Stanley reappeared at the counter's edge, his arms full of chocolate Joe Louis' and strawberry Twinkies.

"And these too," said Bobby as he helped Stanley load them onto the counter.

The woman looked at Stanley and smiled. "Hi buddy, what's your name?"

Stanley didn't say anything, he just looked scared. He turned toward his father for help. "His name is Otis, and he don't talk too much," said Bobby.

"Nice-looking boy," said the woman smiling at Stanley. She tilted her head up and locked her gaze on Bobby McLay's and said, still smiling, "Nice boy like that oughta eat more than just Twinkies for dinner. Can I interest you in a couple of turkey sandwiches, maybe some milk for the boy?"

Bobby looked down at the boy, who just stared back. The woman was waiting. Bobby shuffled his feet. Bobby didn't like to be told what he should be doing, especially from some fat trailer bitch.

"Not a bad idea," said Bobby as he slammed his fist down on the counter. "I'll take two. Otis, go get us a carton of milk."

The woman behind the counter blinked. Bobby knew he had scared her, just a tiny little bit. Just enough.

She moved down to the refrigerated counter, slid the glass door and grabbed some sandwiches wrapped in wax paper.

Stanley came back with a litre of 2% chocolate Sealtest. The woman rang it all up as Pat Sajak, giving the wheel another spin, looked on from the television.

"Thirty-three fifty-six," said the woman.

"Oh yeah, gimme two bags of ice too," said Bobby smiling. "Need to keep my beer cold."

......

The baby-blue K-car, the Coleman camper in tow, rolled to a stop at Lot 61.

"Here we are little man," said Bobby.

"Why did you call me Otis?" asked Stanley, chewing on a Hot Rod.

"You never use your real name when you are undercover. See, you always use an alias when you're hiding out, that way the cops can't easily track your movements. Besides, I wanted to call you Otis from the very beginning, but your mother insisted on Stanley."

Stanley didn't say anything, he just pulled down the plastic wrap and took another bite.

"Come on, I'll show you how the camper works," said Bobby.

Stanley watched as his father turned a crank and the camper slowly came to life like a giant, slow-motion jack-in-the-box. Bobby threw in the metal support bars on either end where the beds jutted out, strode back to Stanley and looped an arm around his shoulder.

"Whaddya think of that pal? Not bad, eh?"

Stanley nodded.

"You remember Uncle Phil?"

"Mommy says that Uncle Phil isn't really my uncle, and that he is a bad man."

"Never you mind your mother. Yeah, technically Phil might not be your uncle, but that don't make him a bad guy. See, me and Phil, eh ... well the reason I wanted you to stay another night, you know, spend some quality time together is on account of Phil and me, well, we've got this job to do and then we are going to be away for a while, lay nice and low, so I got us this camper. So I might not see you for a while Otis."

Stanley squirmed out from under his father's arm.

"I don't like *Otis*, I like *Stanley*."

"Okay, okay, I'm sorry. Stanley it is. Look, it's getting dark, let's build a fire and eat those sandwiches."

"Okay," said Stanley.

......

The smell of sweetgrass filled Bobby's nose when he went over to the cooler to grab himself another Miller High Life. He sat back down on a wooden stump next to where Stanley was chewing on his sandwich.

"What does *incarcerated* mean?" asked Stanley.

Bobby grabbed a long stick from the fire and used the end of it to light a cigarette. "Well, it means being put in jail."

"Mommy says *you* have been incarcerated."

"Yeah, that's right Stanley, and jail is not a place you ever wanna be."

The fire spit and hissed as Bobby poked at it with his stick. A big log rolled over and sprayed a volcano of orange embers into the night sky.

"Bobby, why does the moon get bigger and smaller?" asked Stanley.

"For Christ's sake, don't call me Bobby boy, I'm your father. Call me *Dad* or *Daddy* but not Bobby, okay. Got it?!"

"But Mommy said..."

"I don't give a shit what mommy said, that cocksucker Larry is not your daddy. I'm your daddy. Nobody else is ever goin' be your daddy except me."

Bobby spit into the fire.

"Hey, look at me!" said Bobby.

Stanley looked over like he was expecting a slap. The light of the fire danced across their faces, the deep shadows exaggerating their expressions.

"Shit," said Bobby taking a swig of beer.

They sat in silence for a while, Stanley slowly working on his sandwich, Bobby working on his case of beer.

"I'm full," said Stanley with a quarter of his sandwich left.

Bobby grabbed it out of Stanley's hands and stuffed it into his mouth, muffling to Stanley that he had mustard on his face.

"So, you want to know about the moon do ya?" asked Bobby chewing and swallowing. "Well the moon don't get bigger and smaller, it's the shadow of the earth, see. The moon is like this giant rock rotating around the earth. Shit, don't they teach you nothing in school these days?"

Bobby picked up a big rock.

"Okay, look. The fire is the sun, see, and the beer bottle, we'll pretend it's the earth, okay? Now watch the shadow on the rock as I move it around the beer bottle. See?"

Stanley nodded.

"The moon is still all there, you only get to see a piece of it though, because the earth is casting its shadow on it, get it?"

Stanley nodded again. Bobby tilted back the earth and drained it of its frothy golden oceans.

"You know all them stars up there, well you know what they are don't ya?"

Stanley shook his head.

"Well them stars, they are just like our sun, only they're much further away. As a matter of fact, some of them are so far away that they don't exist anymore. It takes so long for the light to get here, by the time it does, well that fire has long been out."

"Which ones don't exist?" asked Stanley.

"Some of those real tiny ones I think, but I'm not really sure." Bobby lit a smoke.

"Know where the Big Dipper is?" asked Bobby.

Stanley shook his head.

"See them stars there," Bobby said, pointing. "Those three, they make the handle. Those other four stars below, they make the rest of the ladle. Looks like a big soup spoon."

"Wow, that's cool," said Stanley.

Bobby smiled. He got up and got himself another beer.

They watched the stars for a long time. Bobby pointed out different constellations. He explained how the seasons worked, explained shooting stars, and even hashed over the probability of life on other planets. When the fire was close to dying out, Bobby took the last swallow of his beer and told Stanley it was time for bed.

Stanley smelled the strong fumes of alcohol and smoke coming off his father's breath as he kissed him good night.

"Sweet dreams little buddy," slurred Bobby, stumbling to the other side of the camper and hopping into his bed.

Stanley lay still listening to the crickets and the crinkling of the smouldering fire and thought about the stars, and about how big the universe was. He heard his father's breathing become deeper, longer, about to break into a snore.

"Dad?"

Nothing.

"Dad?"

"Huh?" croaked Bobby. "What is it?"

"How long are you going to be gone for?"

"Oh I don't know, maybe a few months, maybe more."

"How many times will the moon wax and..."

"Wane?"

"Yeah."

"A few. Now go to sleep now son."

"Night dad."

"Night son."

Within two minutes Bobby McLay was snoring loudly.

......

When they drove past a four-store strip mall on the outskirts of the city, Bobby slowed right down and took a good look. On the third pass by, Stanley asked where they were going.

"I just need to make a quick stop to buy some smokes."

After ten minutes of circling around on a back road, Bobby pulled off onto the gravel and put on his hazards.

"I'm just going across that field there to go to the store. If anybody approaches the car I want you to honk the horn three times, nice and long. Got it? Three times. Now don't worry, I'll be right back. Keep the doors unlocked and the engine running."

Bobby reached into the back seat and grabbed a small black bag.

Stanley watched his father cross the field toward the back of the building. On the radio the Rolling Stones belted out "Sympathy for the Devil." Halfway through the field his father stopped and put on what looked like a black toque. He also had something shiny in his hand. Soon his father disappeared around the side of the building. Stanley kept staring, his breath fogging the window. He pulled his face back and made a happy face in the vapour. It quickly evaporated. The happy face reappeared when he breathed on the window again. Stanley got lost in this fun.

Bang! Stanley sat up. Fear gripped him. He suspected that was the sound of a gun. His father's gun? He didn't know what had happened, didn't know what he should do. He kept looking across the field for his father, but he wasn't there. Swivelling in his seat, he looked out the back window. Nothing. Nobody there. He waited. Suddenly his father appeared from around the corner of the building. Bobby was running. Fast. He came across the field wearing a black ski mask. Stanley had never seen his father run so fast. He had never seen anyone run so fast.

"Whooooweeeee!" yelled Bobby as he opened the car door.

He tossed his black mask and bag into the back seat and threw a white plastic bag on Stanley's lap. Bobby was grinning from ear to ear. He floored the gas pedal and the wheels spewed gravel.

"Ha! Do me a favour son, count that will ya?" asked Bobby. "And for Christ's sake Stanley, don't tell your mother about this."

Stanley looked at his father, broke into a big smile and shook his head no.

As they approached the city core, Bobby noticed that Stanley, his face contorted while he counted on his fingers, was close to finishing totalling up the loot.

"So, how much we got?"

"Ummm...I think more than five hundred dollars."

"Hot dog!" yelled Bobby as they pulled into the parking lot of a mall.

"Hot dog," repeated Stanley grinning.

"Okay, gimme the money and I'll be right back. Sit tight. Roll down the windows if you get hot," said Bobby, and he was gone.

Stanley noticed he didn't take his black bag or ski mask.

After a while Stanley was bored, so he got his toy car out of his knapsack. Making *brooom brooom* sounds he ran the toy car along the spine of the seat. He drove it along the window's edge, across the duct-taped dashboard, around the steering column, down the other window, flew it through the air, and landed it back at the top of the seat.

The black ski mask and bag sitting in the back seat recaptured Stanley's attention. He put his car down and reached into the back. He put the ski mask on. It was too big, but he managed to align the eyeholes so he could see. He reached into the black bag. Carefully Stanley pulled it out. It was heavy. For several minutes he looked it over, keeping an eye on the door where his father had disappeared. Stanley had been told never to touch it. He put it back. He took off the ski mask and waited. Two minutes later he saw his father coming out of the mall holding a big long box.

......

"I wanted to get you a little something before I go on my trip with Uncle Phil. It's a telescope."

"What's a telescope?"

"It's to look at the stars and the planets at night, just like we did, only you get to see a whole lot more. It comes with this cool star map so you can figure out what you're looking at."

Stanley stared down at the box.

"Mom won't let me keep it."

"What? What do you mean she won't let you keep it?" asked Bobby.

"She'll say it's too expensive and make me take it back to the store."

"That's crap. Don't worry about it, I'll have a word with your mother."

......

When they pulled up to the house the door immediately opened and Marlene stepped out onto the porch, crossed her arms, and waited.

Bobby rolled down his window.

"Hi honey, we're home!" yelled Bobby.

"Stanley, come here baby," said Marlene.

"I'll help you carry your telescope up to the porch. It's pretty heavy," said Bobby to Stanley.

Stanley hung his head low and nodded.

"Don't worry little man, your old man will come back and see you real soon. And until then, you got the stars. And when you look at them you can think of me."

Stanley looked up, smiled slightly, and nodded.

"Stanley!" yelled Marlene.

"Oh Marlene, he's coming for Christ's sake, stop your hollering already."

Bobby took a big breath through his nose and let it out slowly.

"Okay little man, this is it. I'll see you in a while, but don't worry, I'm coming back. Grab your bag and let's go," said Bobby.

Bobby and Stanley walked toward the porch.

"What's that?" demanded Marlene.

"Gift for Stanley," said Bobby.

"What truck did it fall off of?"

"Very funny. It's a telescope, and the receipt is in the box. Bought it this morning. Don't you make him take it back. He's a smart kid. He likes looking at the stars. Don't you Stanley?"

"Look, you're supposed to stay fifty metres away at all times," said Marlene taking a step back.

"Relax, I'll leave it right here and you can take it in. Look, I might be gone for a while."

"You can say that again."

"What's that supposed to mean?" As soon as he asked, Bobby heard the sirens. He turned his head and saw the cruisers coming down both ends of the street.

"Oh, *fuck you* Marlene!" screamed Bobby.

"Stanley, go inside," ordered Marlene.

Stanley bolted down the steps, still wearing his knapsack, yelling that he had forgotten his toy car.

"Stanley, get back here!" screamed Marlene.

"Fucking great, just fucking great Marlene, you really know how to fuck things up!"

Four police cruisers came screeching to a halt, two on the sidewalk, and one on either side of the car and camper.

"Stanley!" screamed Marlene.

"Coming," said Stanley as he ran back across the lawn. "I had to get my car."

Marlene grabbed Stanley and bolted into the house, slamming the front door behind them.

The police got out. Guns were drawn. Bobby was ordered to lay face down on the lawn and clasp his hands behind his head. He didn't resist.

Before he was put into the car, as he was being read his rights, Bobby yelled, "See you in the stars little buddy!"

Stanley appeared in the upper bedroom window. He was holding up his father's black bag. Bobby saw him and gave him a wink and a big smile.

Stanley watched his father sitting in the back seat of the police cruiser, watched until they drove him away.

That night after his mother and stepfather had gone to bed, Stanley climbed out and went over to the window where he had set up his telescope. He scanned the moon. He scanned the stars.

SIX WAYS TO SUNDAY

It was a Sunday. Our souls had been clean and quiet like a church all week. I guess they were looking for some fire and brimstone. So me and Lill stop in for a few short ones over at the Lockmaster. We were just going to have a couple; you know, take it slow and easy like the day itself. Well one leads to another and the next thing I know we got a whole goddamn parade of little draft glasses marching over to our table. The little beast of a devil that is sitting on my shoulder gets all big and tough and full of energy and climbs over my big fat balding head, his little squishy feet feeling like gobs of gooey sweat, and he kicks the little angel on my other shoulder right in the ass. Not what you would call a good Sunday thing to happen.

Then my buddy Ted, who I hadn't seen in forever, shows up out of nowhere, and the three of us set to work playing catch-up. Ted tells all kinds of crazy stories, how he's been in jail, how he got hooked on smack in the slammer, how he got out and went into rehab, how he worked in the guts of a toothpaste factory, and how he got fired for drinking mouthwash on the job. He says he has been drunk ever since.

Now Lill don't say too much. Maybe on account that she and Ted used to date and maybe she still has a thing for him, or maybe on account that she and Ted used to date and she don't want nothing to do with him. Whatever the reason, Lill is quiet. Maybe the draft is calming her down. Lill. So full of energy. Such a woman. Wanders down the streets and does four loads of laundry, comes back and attacks the stack of barbarian dishes that have invaded the sink. Then vacuums, cleans the ashtrays, goes and gets real food, cooks it and presents it by tablecloth and candlelight with a bottle of good wine. Lill. After all that, still a tiger in the sack. That was Saturday.

So Ted, full of crooked teeth and draft, wants to play pool. There are some big Natives playing. Ted waddles over and puts a loonie on the edge of the table.

When the black ball goes down, the big chief wearing a leather tasselled jacket waves. "Wanna play doubles, you and your friend?" he asks.

What I haven't told you about Ted is, despite being a fucked-up alcoholic low-life with no job and no prospects, the man is a shark. Even when he is blotto, he plays pool better than anyone I've ever seen. He's like Paul Newman in that movie, you know the one. Like that, though maybe not quite that good. But almost.

Ted smiles his broken piano key smile and gives me a big wink. "Doug, you wanna play?"

I look at Lill and she nods okay, she doesn't mind being left alone for a bit.

Introductions go around and this mean-looking Indian named Lee cracks the balls wide open and starts going after the solids like they were buffalo. Pow, pow, pow. He kills three of them, but just wounds the fourth, kissing off the corner pocket.

Then Ted's up. Sinks two and just misses an easy third.

"Well shit," says Ted.

The big chief is next. He clears the rest of the solids, except for the eight ball—that rattles in the side pocket and doesn't go in.

"Not looking good for the good guys," says Ted as I chalk up my cue.

I bang in two more of our balls, and then Lee comes back and finishes us off. Lee smiles for the first time.

"Okay, whattillit be boys, a round of Blues?" I ask, seeing as they are drinking the stuff.

They both nod. The bartender brings over the beers. Lill comes over and we switch to a spot closer to the pool table.

"Wanna play again?" asks Ted, looking over at the chief.

"Okay, but how about ten bucks this time, seein' as we have lots of beer?"

"Hey, you guys are good. Doug, what do you think, ten bucks too rich for your blood?"

Lill leans over and whispers in my ear, tells me she doesn't like this, that she has a bad feeling about these guys.

I nod.

"Okay, sure, let's do it," says Ted. "Except let's make it twenty."

......

Lee breaks again. The guy has a powerhouse break. Balls everywhere. That's it, he's gone. Runs the table clean. Impressive. I fork over the twenty bucks. Lee smiles for the second time.

Now I'm starting to think, who's conning who here? I know Ted can take him, but will we get a second chance? Payday is not until Thursday and I only got twenty bucks left, after I just paid Lee. And I want to keep drinking. I know Lill has a thirst on. She is pounding them back. Plus we are running out of smokes.

"Wanna play again?" asks Ted.

"Twenty bucks?" asks the chief.

"Double or nothing, how 'bout forty?"

The chief glances at Lee. Lee smiles for the third time.

Lee explodes the balls again and sinks two stripes right off. The zebra hunter goes to work. Pow, pow, pow. Next thing I know I'm watching Lee smoke the eight ball in the corner pocket and Ted and I are each reaching for our last twenty bucks.

Let me say this, Ted didn't even blink when Lee asked if we wanted to play again for eighty. Ted said, let's make it a hundred. Lee smiled for the fourth and last time.

Swack! Lee busts 'em wide apart, but this time nothing falls.

"Cutting the good guys a break," says Ted.

He grabs the blue chalk off the edge of the table. He takes his time. Chalking his cue, eyeing the table, weighing all the options, Ted moves slowly around the table. He bends down a few times and squints at a couple of balls.

Ted stands up straight and says, pointing with his cue, "Okay, six in the corner." And with that, he's off.

When the eight ball slowly trickles into the pocket, Ted smiles his pearly off-whites and Lee scowls and asks if we want another go.

"Well now, you and the chief there, you guys are pretty good. I don't know. How about the best of seven games, three hundred bucks, winners take all, then we call it a day?"

Lee leans over and whispers something into the chief's ear and the chief nods.

"Okay," says the chief. "But we flip a coin to see who goes first."

I look at Ted and he nods.

"Okay, heads or tails?"

They win the toss and Lee clears the table, again. Lill gives me a dirty look. I shrug my shoulders as if to say, what, there's no problem here, but I'm thinking, Christ, how are we going to pay? My palms are moist.

Lee starts the second game by sinking both a coloured and a striped off the break. He bangs a few balls in and finally misses. Ted is up and finishes off game two, then three, and misses in the fourth. The chief takes care of business, runs the table like a bad dog, but blows the break in the fifth. So I'm up. I manage three balls and hook myself behind the eight. I call safety and lightly bounce the cue ball off the rail to land it right back where it started, nestled behind the eight. Now, some people might call that dirty pool. Three hundred bucks and no way to pay, I call it smart.

Lee is back up. Slam-Bam, there goes game five. Now we are in a pickle. We just need a little bit of luck. Lee fires off his crackerjack break and three balls drop, including the cue. Our little bit of luck.

Off Ted goes. I breathe a sigh of relief when I see that eight ball drop and game six is ours.

I go over to where Lill is sitting and rub her shoulders. She seems rather tense.

"How you doing babe?"

"Christ Doug, I can't take the tension," says Lill and then lowers her voice, "What are you going to do if you lose?"

"Think positive baby."

Ted breaks and sinks two solids. He drops three more, but misses on the five ball. But Ted is good. Even when he misses, he leaves them nothing. All the chief can see is our seven ball. That Ted, always getting good position.

The chief takes his time. He moves slowly around the table, twice. My palms are rivers and somebody is tattooing a butterfly on the inside of my stomach. God almighty.

The chief calls two banks, nine in the corner. He leans down and I can hear the scrunching sound of his leather jacket. He lightly taps it, one bank, two banks, taps the nine and it rolls gently toward the corner and stops. Stops, right on the lip.

The chief lets out a groan.

"Wow," says Ted smiling. "Is this a goddamn nail-biter or what?"

Lee's facial expression doesn't change. Instead, he pulls out a cellphone, dials a number, waits, speaks about five words in some Native language and hangs up and says, as wooden as a totem pole, "Your shot."

Ted passes me the cue. Three hundred bucks. Damn. Five, seven and the eight ball. I look over at Lill and she nods her head and smiles, like she was saying, go get 'em baby.

Well half this game is sinking your ball; the other half is lining up your next shot. The five ball is no problem; it's getting to the seven that's the trouble. I drop the five and the cue ball sort of stops, then it starts coming back. I put all the backspin on that little sucker that my warped cue can muster. It's perfect I tell you, perfect. I drop the seven ball. But I'm not thinking clear. Maybe it's the draft, maybe it's the smell of money that close, or maybe I just want to impress Lill. I don't really think about getting good position for the eight. I leave myself a one-bank-in-the-side and not much else. When I ask Ted what he thinks, he purses his lips and sucks air slowly through his nose and says, "I think you better hurry up and sink it."

So I'm lining up for my shot when the door opens and these two big Indians, the size of bears, come lurching into the bar, their long black hair pulled back in tight ponytails. Lee says something to them in his native tongue and these two refrigerators sit down at a table eye-level across from where I'm shooting. When I give them a friendly smile, as I hunch over the cue ball, they remain perfectly still. They have gold rings on every finger and tattoos up their arms.

"One bank in the side," I say as I cock my cue back and fire.

When the eight ball falls, Ted's lips part, giving way to his smile of jagged and twisted teeth. "Nice work Doug," he says as he pats me on the shoulder. I look over at Lill and she raises her glass up in salutation. Lee counts out the money on the table in three piles of hundreds. "Thanks very much," says Ted, and as he goes to grab it off the table Lee grabs his wrist.

"These boys want to play you for four hundred dollars," says Lee, still holding Ted's arm.

"Well now," says Ted, "how about if I don't feel like playing anymore?"

Lee doesn't say anything. The two big Indians stand up. Ted smiles.

"Okay, how about five hundred?" asks Ted.

Lee lets go of Ted's arm. They stare each other down.

"Okay, five hundred," says Lee finally.

"Let's have a smoke break first, shall we?" I ask.

"Good idea Doug, and maybe a round of beer," Ted adds.

"Lill, go get some smokes will ya?" I say as I pass her a twenty and bend down to give her a kiss on the cheek. I whisper quickly and quietly into her ear to get a cab and have it waiting on the corner, that we'll be out in five minutes.

I order two pitchers of beer, one for us and one for them. When the waiter brings them over, I pay and pour Ted and I each a glass. I down half of mine and ask Ted if he will join me outside for a smoke. Ted says sure, and as we head for the door, Lee says to make sure that we come back.

"Leave a full pitcher of beer behind, are you nuts?" I say and push Ted to hurry him out the door.

I see the Blue Line Taxi cab sitting there idle and Lill peering out the back window. She waves.

"Time to go," I say to Ted.

"Hey, don't you want to play those guys?" asks Ted while we both start to jog toward the cab.

"Very funny," I say.

We pile into the cab and I tell the driver to go to the King Edward liquor store. The cabbie pulls a U-ey and just as we pass by the side door of the bar, out steps Lee with his two big linebackers, Chuckles and Smiley. Lee realizes that it's us in the cab and starts yelling and pointing.

Meanwhile the cabbie has slowed down and stopped further up the block because some jackass is parallel parking in slow motion. Out the back window we can see them running toward us. "We got to get going man!" I yell to the cabbie.

The cabbie, a Sikh with a blue turban, says he doesn't want any trouble. I tell him if he doesn't want any trouble, he better get his ass moving or those guys running down the block are going to give it to him, big time. The cabbie takes one look in his mirror and pulls into the oncoming lane and around the blocking car. Ted rolls down the window, leans his upper body out and flips them the finger while screaming, "See you later, fuckers!"

......

Ted gives the cabbie a five-dollar tip and me my half of the money. We buy a forty of Wild Turkey, eighteen tallboys of Old Milwaukee, and a bottle of sparkling wine to celebrate our good fortune.

When we get out of the liquor store, it starts to rain. So we hurry home. Lill and I rent the last house in a six-row unit. It's not much, but it's all we can afford. Lill works the lunch counter in a government building. I'm the janitor. That's how we met.

Anyway, we get in out of the rain with Ted still in tow and we set to work drinking. Ted pops the bubbly and smiles explode all over our faces.

"Here's to kicking their asses!" says Ted holding up my Esso coffee mug full of wine.

"Did you see their faces?" asks Lill. "That was priceless."

After the bubbly I pour three large bourbons and get us some beers to chase 'em down. The rain starts to come down hard and we match it with our drink. We play some cards and we tell stories of when we were younger, had bigger dreams, and had bodies that were more limber.

Now when Lill gets drinking, for some reason or other she likes to get chatty with her girlfriends. So about 10:30 she says excuse me, I need to make a call. Ted knows the routine too; after all they used to go out.

Near midnight I lend Ted a coat and a half busted umbrella to make a dash over to his place, which just happens to be six blocks away, to get some more beer. Once you're in a groove, it's hard to stop. Ted comes back in half an hour, half drowned, and announces that he's got half a twelve-pack and a half finished twenty-sixer of Jamaican over-proof rum.

"Well on the whole," I say, "I think you did darn well." We laugh. We pour more drinks. Lill comes in still gabbing happily on the portable and refreshes her drink. Then there is CRASH, and then SMASH and BANG, SLAM, CRASH.

Ted and I both look out the window. I can see my neighbour Bill fighting with his garbage can in the rain, drunk as a skunk. Since his wife left, Bill is always drunk as a skunk. And he is always locking himself out of his house.

So now Bill is throwing garbage all over his lawn, shaking the can upside down. "What the Christ is he doing?" asks Ted.

"I think he has locked himself out again, and he is taking it out on the garbage can."

"Really?"

"Yeah, really."

When Bill finally manages to get all the garbage out, he places the garbage can over his head, sits down and leans up against a parking sign. There Bill is, feet sticking out from underneath the can like some sort of cartoon, like a man who has been beaten up.

"Or maybe he just wanted a dry place to sleep?" I suggest to Ted.

"Could be," says Ted, "could be."

......

It's nearing one in the morning and Ted says he ought to get going home.

"One more for the road?" I ask, getting up to get a beer from the fridge.

"Okay," says Ted. "Just one more."

I pass Ted a beer. As he pops the cap, Lill comes in with tears rolling down her face.

"What's the matter?" I ask.

"I was talking to Pam," she says.

Pam is her sister. She is two years younger than Lill and just had her third kid.

"Yes," I say, "and what?"

"I'm thirty-six Doug."

"And so what?" I ask.

"Doug, I'm thirty-six. Thirty-*SIX*!" she screams, "I'm thirty-six! Thirty-six, thirty-six, thirty-six!"

Ted puts down his beer and says quietly that he really needs to get going home, that it's late.

I shake his hand and thank him for the great time.

"Yeah, Ted, thanks a fucking lot!" yells Lill.

"Hey, Jesus Christ, what the hell's gotten into you?" I ask.

"Bye," says Ted and closes the door behind him.

"I'm thirty-six Doug!"

"For Christ's sake, stop saying that! I know you're thirty-six. What about it?"

"I want a baby! I WANT A BABY!"

"Do you think we're ready for that?" I ask calmly and take a sip of my beer.

"Doug, are you listening to me?" asks Lill softly, then screams, "I WANT A FUCKING BABY!!"

And with that she throws the portable with all her might against the wall. It explodes into pieces.

I don't say anything. I just get up, put my arm around her shoulder. She lets me walk her to bed.

......

When I get up in the morning, I throw up in the toilet. I look at my eyes in the mirror. They hold the devil's stain—bloodshot. I know I can't make it in to work. So I go downstairs and there is the phone in pieces. I put on shoes and a bathrobe and cross the street to the payphone and call my boss.

On my way back I notice Bill's no longer in his garbage can and the front window of his house is wide open. I shake Lill awake and hand her a quarter to use the phone so she can call in sick too.

We spend most of the day sleeping it off. After bathing and a late lunch, tuna fish sandwiches and dill pickle chips, I take Lill to the bedroom. I hump her six ways to Sunday. I give her everything. I give her all my seed.

THE PINEAPPLE THAI VILLAGE

The Squid's hands were moving fast and furiously, ripping dishes and spoons out of a grey overflowing bus-pan; dishes covered with leftover greasy nicotine noodles, coconut curry sauces, and peanut satay cigarette juice. In a rapid, fluid motion, the Squid popped the dishes into a red rack with a slam, slam, slam, clink, clink, clink. Watching the Squid work was like watching a great ballroom dancer. And Harry, the silver beast of a dishwashing machine, was a great dancing partner to have. Harry's timing was impeccable, and the Squid had his movements down cold. The Squid and Harry danced like Fred Astaire and Ginger Rogers. They were the best dishwashing team the Pineapple Thai Village had ever known.

Filling the rack, the Squid hit the dishes with the T-spray. BANG, up went the door and out came a cloud of steam: clean rack out, dirty rack in, close the door and hit the switch back on. The Squid wiped his wet dirty hands on his sauce-stained apron and took a drag off his illegally imported Marlboro cigarette, which he left burning in an ashtray atop Harry. He unloaded Harry, filled a new rack of dishes, hit them with the T-spray and had a drag of his smoke all before Harry finished his three-minute cycle: BANG, door up, steam, clean rack out, dirty rack in, door down, hit the switch, have a drag, unload, reload, spray, BANG, door up, steam, clean rack out, dirty rack in, door down, hit the switch, have a drag... The Squid was good, he had a system.

Thongchai was staring at a sea of little yellow papers and trying to remember if he had given table sixteen their spring rolls. BANG, Su-Li came through the swinging kitchen doors with a panicked swirling energy, like she couldn't find her car keys ten minutes before an important job interview, or like the fifty-year-old neurotic that she was.

"Where my spring roll?" asked Su-Li as she slapped her hand on the serving area next to the small bell used to signal a food pick-up.

"Shit. Forgot," said Thongchai with a big dumb, goofy grin. He pivoted on one of his greasy black running shoes toward the walk-in refrigerator to retrieve the spring rolls.

"Dese people waiting fifteen minute ahready! How come you no good? What you doing? You do the play, you never do the work," yelled Su-Li at Thongchai over the frying noise of Rocket Ray's three woks and Harry's loud, chugging, gurgling whirl. Then Su-Li turned toward the Squid to give him a piece of her mind too. The Squid was leaning back on Harry, already grinning at Su-Li, smoking his cigarette.

"We need da spoon. No spoon, no spoon," squealed Su-Li. "You no good, you smoking ahways, never do the work."

The Squid started to move toward Su-Li, and she immediately started to back up.

"Cutlery! It's cutlery!" yelled the Squid as he grabbed a fork and started to brandish it in the direction of Su-Li's head.

"See this?" continued the Squid on his rant, much to the amusement of Thongchai and Rocket Ray.

"This is a fork. It's not a spoon, it's not a knife. It's a fork."

"You no threaten me! I tell Sheena you threaten me! You work here no more when I tell Sheena!"

"What are you going to say? *Squid point spoon at me, Squid point spoon?*"

"I know fork, I know bucket!"

"Yeah, and *you* no good! It's a spoon, not a bucket!"

"I telling Sheena, you no good!"

"How 'bout I jab this up your ass and try and pull out the pickle? Why don't you get the hell out of the kitchen and quit bothering people? Why don't you go neurotically polish your spoons?"

Su-Li scooted around the Squid.

"I telling Sheena," she said as she went, BANG, back out through the swinging doors of the kitchen.

Rocket Ray, covered in Chinese dragon tattoos and clad in blue jeans, a wife-beater undershirt, a dirty apron and a small white paper cap, was laughing his ass off.

"You are going to make her have a breakdown," said Rocket Ray, while he continued to individually spice each separate dish in the three woks like he was painting juggling balls while they were in the air.

"I was hoping for an aneurysm."

Thongchai finished putting the last details on his cucumber penguins used to decorate table five's appetizer platter, then he hit the bell for a pick-up.

BING, BING, BING.

BANG, Sarah marched through the swinging kitchen doors with so much confidence that you would have thought that she had an army behind her. Her mother was dark Thai and her father was light Canadian. Sarah had the best features of both. She was a stunner, and the Squid was in love with her.

"Nice penguins Thong," remarked Sarah as she grabbed the appetizer platter.

The Squid was admiring her figure—definitely not a penguin. "So Sarah, you are a psychology student right?" asked the Squid. "Tell me, what do you see in that Rorschach ink-blob boyfriend of yours anyway?"

Sarah turned quickly to the Squid, causing one of the penguins to waddle precariously close to the edge of the plate she was carrying.

"Hey Squid, why don't you leave poor Glen alone for a night?" asked Sarah with a half smile, like she somehow enjoyed the Squid's badmouthing and insults.

"I'll leave poor Glen alone when you dump his ugly ass and go out with me. I mean the guy carries that briefcase like a Neanderthal carries a club. I mean for the love of God, doesn't that tell you something?"

BING, Thongchai hit the bell.

BANG, Su-Li came barrelling through the kitchen doors, grabbed her spring rolls without looking at or saying anything to anyone, and BANG, back out the doors she went.

"It tells me that you're extremely jealous," said Sarah smiling, as BANG, she went out the kitchen doors with the appetizer platter for table five, penguins and all.

The Squid stood there with his hands on his hips looking at Thongchai and Rocket Ray for some kind of response. With a quick flick of the wrist, the Squid pulled out a small black plastic comb from his back pocket and started to adjust his retro duck-tailed Elvis do.

"I mean, what's wrong with me? I'm charming, good looking, smart. I mean what's this girl thinking? Glen? Glen is what?
Glen is charming like gum disease, that's what. A gum disease
that drives a Jeep, who is probably sitting around right now as I
speak, trying to figure out which fucking silk shirt matches his
watered-down personality."

"You're also only eighteen," said Rocket Ray as he trans-
ferred food from wok to serving bowl.

"I'm going to be nineteen next month. Sarah is what,
twenty-four, twenty-five?"

"Twenty-five."

"So what Ray? I mean come on, that's what, only seven
years. Seven years. What's seven years? When I'm thirty, she'll
be thirty-seven. When I'm fifty, she'll be fifty-seven. When I'm
ninety, she'll be ninety-seven. Do you see what I'm saying here?
Calculus man, calculus is what I'm talking about. When those
two lines approach infinity, do you know what the difference
is? Nothing is the difference. Absolutely nothing."

"Glen is also a Chinese dentist, and you, my friend, are a
white dish-pig."

"What the hell you talkin' about Ray? Who had to drive
Sarah home the other night because our buddy Glen got pissed
with his frat boys and forgot to pick her up? You. You had
to drive her home, so don't give me that dentist shit. I'm one
charming dude. And charm lasts longer than teeth."

BING. Rocket Ray hit the bell for a pick-up. "I'm charming too," said Ray showing off his tombstone teeth. "More
charming than you might think," as he continued to give the
Squid a mocking smile.

"Ray, I'm talking about love, man. Love and calculus,

points on a curve." said the Squid while he moved back toward Harry, making an hour-glass shape in the air with his hands. Thongchai laughed at the Squid's hand movements like he was an embarrassed teenager in sex-ed class.

BANG. Sarah came roaring back in and started to grab her food for table one. The Squid moved around her and put his hands on her shoulders and said, "I love this girl, and it's only a matter of time before she loves me back."

"Two words," said Sarah in a cold tone. "Sexual harassment."

The Squid backed off with his hands raised like a bank teller at gunpoint. "What's wrong there Sarah, got a loose filling? Do you think Glen can really fill your cavities?"

Sarah looked at Rocket Ray, turned with her food, and BANG, went out the kitchen door. BANG, Sheena came walking in. "Squid we need to talk."

......

Two hours later the Squid was mopping the bathroom floors. The Squid had noticed where the tile was lifting up from too much bleach—just like my heart, thought the Squid, too much Sarah. And away he went, working that squeeze lever on the mop bucket with the same grace and control he had when he danced with Harry. Squeeze, dunk, splat, mop, squeeze, dunk, splat, mop. The Squid was good, he had a system.

An hour later, after the grease traps had been cleaned and Harry had been put to bed for the night, the Squid sat at table eighteen with a plate of rice and curry watching in awe as Thongchai chewed his food with his mouth open, little bits of rice and lemon chicken falling like the first snowfall of winter.

"Thong, that's just plain foul man. Chew with your mouth closed," said the Squid. Thongchai ignored the Squid, like he usually did, and proceeded to suck the marrow out of a skinny chicken bone, producing a sound like he was trying to play a broken wind instrument.

Sarah was sitting at the next table going through her slips and money. Sheena was at the bar doing her own cash-out.

"Have a good night Sarah?" asked Sheena.

"Excellent. It hasn't been that busy for weeks."

"Only to be spoiled by the presence of Dr. Novocaine when he comes to pick you up," said the Squid as he popped a fork decorated with beef and pineapple into his mouth.

"Squid, that's what I'm talking about with Su-Li," said Sheena. "You antagonize and pick fights."

"I'm just having a little fun."

Sarah got up and handed Sheena her receipts and a pile of cash. "Sometimes you don't know when to quit Squid," said Sarah with genuine hurt in her voice, as she headed for the kitchen doors. BANG, and she was gone.

"What's got into her? I can't help that Glen is a boring asshole."

"You ahways talking. Why you don't eat with mouth closed?" said Thongchai as he gave a cold stare to the Squid. The Squid stared back in bewilderment.

Ting, ting, ting. The Squid's shoulders raised and he grimaced as he heard the familiar sound of Glen's tapping against the restaurant's front window. Sheena moved around the bar and headed for the front door to let him in. The Squid started shovelling beef and pineapple into his mouth rapidly—the less time he had to sit and talk with Glen the better.

"Hi Thong. Hi Squid," said Glen with a friendly tooth-paste grin, as he sat down with his ever-present briefcase at the next table.

Thongchai acknowledged him with a nod while he worked on another chicken bone.

"Hey Glen, Sarah is in the kitchen, I'll go get her for you," said the Squid as he scooped the last of his curry and rice into his mouth, got up with his empty plate and started to head for the kitchen.

"Thanks Squid."

"Don't mention it Glen," said the Squid, as BANG, the Squid's world inverted.

......

Time slowed down and the kitchen got much smaller. Sarah's hands were locked onto the tattooed muscular biceps of Rocket Ray, as she was open-mouth kissing him, leaning up against the grill. The Squid saw Rocket Ray in a darker light, a light of betrayal. He looked older and meaner, and Sarah looked like somebody had taken the Ferris wheel out of her spirit. They were both frozen looking at the Squid, waiting for something to happen, waiting for the silence to end.

"Glen's here."

"Tell him... Tell him I'll be right out," said Sarah as her voiced wavered.

"Sure thing," said the Squid as he grabbed his smokes off the top of Harry and, BANG, went out the kitchen door. He moved toward Glen. The Squid never would have guessed he could feel sorry for Glen.

"She'll be out in a minute. Do you want to lock me out at the front?"

"Sure. You're not getting a ride with Ray?" asked Glen as he started to follow the Squid to the front door.

"No, tonight I feel like walking. Ever have those nights where you just want to walk?"

"Sure, but it's a long walk isn't it?"

"Not long enough." And the Squid stepped out into the warm summer night and heard the click as Glen locked the door behind him. The Squid lit up another cigarette and took a large drag. He blew the smoke out and said, "Fuck it."

The Squid started walking home, counting the number of steps on the way. The Squid was good, he had a system, and the calculus of time was on his side.

LUCKY BREAK

As their tenth wedding anniversary celebration wound down, Rose giggled in soft protest that they shouldn't, that they had told the sitter that they would be back by twelve, and it was already a quarter after.

"Come on baby, just one last drink. We'll be quick about it. Besides, we never go out on the town," Jim said, arm wrapped around her shoulder as he marched her across the street, away from the moonlight, through the door and into the soft lighting of the Scottsdale Tavern.

They grabbed stools at the counter and Jim ordered a couple bottles of Bud. Loretta Lynn played on the jukebox. A middle-aged couple slowly waltzed nearby. In the corner a couple of men were shooting a game of pool. Jim said that he had to take a piss, that he would be right back. Rose watched his muscular frame swagger toward the can, watched that tight butt in those blue jeans. He was twenty pounds heavier than when they had met, but he was really only a boy then, having just turned fifteen. She had put on thirty pounds. She had tried and tried to shed the weight after the kids, but couldn't. Jim didn't seem to mind though. He still made love to her ferociously after the kids had been put to bed—when they weren't both exhausted from a day's work.

She took a swig of her beer and looked around. The machine was on the corner of the bar. It was cycling through its intro gaming menus when Rose spotted it. She dug into her pocket and pulled out a toonie. She slipped the coin into the mouth of the machine and it chimed gleefully in response. A welcoming menu popped up with her two-dollar credit displayed in the upper right hand corner. Rose selected the 'jungle theme' and hit the spin button. The simulated reels of a slot machine began to spin. Monkeys, alligators and toucans; red, blue and gold stars; bananas, pineapples and oranges all went blurring by. She whacked away at the yellow illuminated buttons at the base of the screen halting the reels one by one. Two blue stars and a monkey. The credit display now read $1.50. She hit the spin button again. Jim came up from behind her. "We rich yet?" he asked, lighting a cigarette and taking a swig off his bottle.

With a whack, whack, whack she nailed the buttons.

An alligator. A blue star. An orange.

"Nope," she replied, hitting spin.

A red star. A banana. A blue star.

"Last one," she said.

Jim spun her in her stool and kissed her on the mouth. "For luck," he said, and turned her back toward to the machine.

Spin. Whack, whack, whack.

Three bug-eyed monkeys with their tails curved over their heads stared at Rose as the machine rang out tinny notes of victory. At the top of the screen "winner" flashed in multicolour. "Waaaahhooooooo!" cried Rose.

"How much did we win baby?" asked Jim, peering over her shoulder.

"Three hundred dollars! Three monkeys is three hundred dollars!"

"Fantastic!" cried Jim.

The bartender, a tall bald man, came over drying a glass with a towel. "You won did you?" he asked.

"How do I get the money?" asked Rose, grinning from ear to ear.

"Just hit the payout key and it'll print you out a ticket. Give it to me and I'll pay you."

Just before Rose hit the payout key her hand froze, hovering an inch over it.

"What's wrong baby? Why don't you hit the button?" asked Jim.

"Maybe we should play just a few more rounds, you know, while luck is with us."

"No baby, we gotta take the money and run. You can get those nice shoes you wanted."

"Yeah, you're right," she agreed and hit the payout key. The machine made some electronic gargling sounds and spit out a ticket.

When the bartender came back and counted out the fifteen twenties on the bar, Jim ordered three shots of JD—one each for Rose, the bartender and himself. "Here's to three monkeys!" toasted Jim, clinking his shot glass against the others. He downed his shot and slammed his glass upside down on the bar.

"Cheers," said the bartender, draining his shot.

......

When they got home Rose tipped the sitter an extra five dollars and insisted that Jim walk her home, even though she lived only a block and a half away.

After checking that the kids were still sleeping soundly, Rose went quickly into the bedroom, squeezed herself into the sausage skin of the red-lace teddy that Jim had bought her. The boning dug into her ribs. She put on fishnet stockings and looked at herself in the mirror.

"God," she muttered, "how can Jim love the likes of this? Christ, I look like a fat Christmas ornament."

"Mom, is that you?" asked a sleepy voice from the hall.

Rose jumped and spun around to see her son Kiel standing in the doorway, pyjamas stained dark at the crotch and top of the legs.

"I wet the bed."

"Oh sweetie. Okay, take off your clothes and put them in the hamper. Put on something dry and Mommy will be there in a minute to change the sheets."

"What are you wearing?"

"Special pyjamas," answered Rose, covering up quickly with her bathrobe.

Kiel smiled slyly and said, "I don't think so."

"Never you mind mom's pyjamas, you hurry up now and change out of those wet things before your father gets home and sees the mess you made."

......

Rose was closing the door to Kiel's room, arms full of wet bedding when she felt Jim's strong hands come around and cup her breasts. She smelled Budweiser and cigarettes as he kissed her on the neck. "Hang on there baby, let me put these away."

"He have another accident?"

"Yeah."

Jim dropped his hands and looked at the hallway floor. "Maybe we should take him to the doctor."

"I've already checked it out. Don't worry, he'll grow out of it," said Rose as she dumped the sheets down the laundry chute.

Jim continued to look despairingly at the floor. He was the embodiment of masculinity, so Rose knew that it must be killing him to have a son so soft, so fragile. A bed-wetter.

She tiptoed down the hall, stood in the doorway of the bedroom and called out to Jim, "Hey lover."

He looked up.

She dropped the bathrobe.

He dropped his jaw.

......

Rose always considered herself fortunate when it came to sex, more so than most of her girlfriends whom she was horrified to learn had never climaxed during intercourse. She could usually achieve orgasm through penetration alone; however, tonight Jim's drunken jackhammer whisky-dick style was doing nothing for her, except making her raw and sore. The digital clock on the nightstand indicated that he had been pumping away for close to forty minutes.

"Come on baby, come and give it to me baby!" Rose cried out.

Jim groaned and continued to thrust away. Over his shoulder she watched his cute round white ass rise and fall rhythmically to his panting. She briefly entertained expediting the process by ramming her finger up his arse as she had done once before. It had worked like a charm, he had cum lickity split, but after he had berated her and told her never to do that again. That kind of thing was for homosexuals, faggots, he had said.

"Oh yes baby, come on, cum baby, cum!" cried out Rose in the best earth-shattering voice she could muster.

When Jim rolled off, he kissed her sweetly and told her that he loved her. A minute after that, he was snoring loudly. She managed to yank herself out of the teddy and inspected the little red indents in her flesh where the boning had dug in.

She lay there. Her drunken mind wandered all over. She thought about how she would need to buy her daughter Tammy new skates. She thought about how good the lobster was they had at dinner. She slithered her tongue about her gums and thought she could still taste a little garlic butter. She thought about the three monkeys. She couldn't wait to get her new shoes. But what if she had kept playing, maybe she could have won a whole lot more?

She rolled over on her belly and masturbated until she was satisfied, then fell asleep. She dreamed of the machine. She dreamed about the monkeys.

......

On Monday, after the kids had been packed off to school with
bellies full of Cheerios and brown-bag lunches stowed in their
knapsacks, Rose vacuumed the house, folded two loads of
laundry and set out to the mall to get her treasure, her red
floral Camper shoes.

She backed out of the driveway and headed down the
street. She turned right and drove two blocks and stopped
at the red light. She looked left, looked at the glow of the
Labatt Blue sign in the window of the Scottsdale Tavern.
Just then its red mouth of a door opened and spit out three
businessmen in suits like watermelon seeds. She looked at her
watch—11:50. She hadn't had any lunch. She had planned on
grabbing something at the mall, but maybe she could grab
a sandwich at the Tavern, maybe play a game or two on the
machine. Besides, she had nothing else planned for the afternoon. When the light turned green, she pulled into the first
available parking spot.

......

It was so much brighter in there during the day, noisy. Crews
of mostly men, four to six, sat around eating lunch—meatball sandwiches, chili, subs. The bartender from the other
night wasn't there. A blonde with large breasts and a ready-
to-please smile had replaced him. Two other women clad in
black miniskirts and cleavage-revealing tank tops worked the
floor with trays of beer. There was a free stool at the bar, near
the machine.

"What can I get you?" asked the blonde when Rose sat down.

"Um, I'll have a diet Coke and a menu please."

"Coming up. Specials are on the chalkboard over there, the soup is tomato."

"Thanks," said Rose. She decided on the grilled chicken club, but got salad instead of fries. When her food arrived, the man with the Detroit Red Wings jacket who was sitting at the machine finally got up to leave. Rose thought he was never going to go.

"I'm just going to move over there," said Rose to the bartender.

"No problem. Just leave it sweetie, I'll move your food over for you."

"Thanks," said Rose.

....

A digital cartoon played on screen of the VLT. Rose was transfixed. She sat there holding a wedge of club sandwich like a cardboard advertisement. She watched as the pixellated monkey pulled the lever of a slot machine. When the monkey won, bananas erupted like a volcano from the top of the slot machine. The monkey danced around in victory. Then the monkey ended up on a beach, like rich millionaire monkeys do, with his stack of bananas beside him. A sexy female monkey brought him his drink and he lifted his sunglasses up and gave a wink to Rose.

Rose put back her sandwich wedge, without having taken a bite, and fished for a twenty from her purse. The VLT emitted a tiny electronic whirling noise as it gulped down the twenty into its guts. Rose hit the spin button.

......

Most of the lunch crowd had emptied out of The Scottsdale. The bartender came by and grabbed Rose's wicker lunch basket and realized it was untouched. "Something wrong with the food honey?"

"Huh?" said Rose, turning her head away from the machine.

"Something wrong with the food?"

Rose noted Vicki's nametag.

"Ah no, just lost track of time playing this thing, just leave it there and I'll eat it in a minute."

Vicki paused and then said, "You know, you ought to be careful with that thing, it can be addictive—real addictive."

Rose turned completely away from the machine, looked Vicki in the eye and smiled her friendliest smile. "You're right," she said, picking up a sandwich wedge and taking a big bite.

"That's a girl, don't let that machine take all your money sweetie. You mind if I settle up with you, I got to get to my other job."

"No, not at all. How much do I owe you, Vicki?"

......

Rose was hungrier than she thought. She ate quickly. She thought about what Vicki had said: addictive. Rose had been playing for only forty-five minutes and was down sixty dollars.

Now she didn't have money for both her shoes and Tammy's skates. But she was due for a big hit. Just twenty more dollars, she thought, and then she would quit either way. She was just going to win back her sixty dollars and leave straight away. Fair and square.

......

It was raining now. The windows of the Corolla were fogged up. Rose stared at the pair of miniature plastic ice skates that hung off the rearview mirror and listened to the rain pound the roof. She popped the glove compartment and fished out a pack of Jim's smokes. With shaky hands she tore off the cellophane and foil wrap and plucked one from the pack. She lit it and inhaled deeply. When she exhaled she was dizzy. Just then, through the smoke, fog and rain, Rose saw the man with the Detroit Red Wings jacket run by her car, heading across the street for the Scottsdale Tavern. She rolled down her window and stuck her head out.

"Hey! That's my money you are going to win, asshole!" screamed Rose, but the rain drowned out her voice and the man didn't seem to hear her as he slipped inside the bar.

Rose took another big long drag. Her hand was shaking. She realized that she was going to be sick. After she puked in the street, she shut the car door and leaned her wet head back against the seat rest and shut her eyes. She listened to the rain.

Rose had grown up on a farm. She'd loved sitting on the porch swing, curled up in a blanket, watching the rain pour down. She remembered one storm in particular, when she was a little girl. She had seen *The Wizard of Oz* on TV and desperately wanted to be Dorothy, desperately wanted to travel to Oz. It was a hot summer day and Rose was alone at the house. Her mother had gone into town to get a dress; her father was down in the barn working on the tractor. She sat on the porch swing and sipped at her lemonade. She rocked back and forth making the tiniest squeak. When she stuck her legs out straight and pointed her toes she could just manage to touch the railing and continue to propel herself. But something was off. Something was strange. Everything seemed so still, quiet. That's when she had seen it. A black line that stretched the length of the horizon. The line quickly grew thick and fat and soon a dark blanket hung across the sky. The darkness was moving toward Rose.

She had run inside to gather her yellow raincoat and boots, her grandfather's floppy fishing hat, which was much too big for her, and her teddy bear with white paws, Spats. She'd quickly made Spats some impromptu rain gear out of a couple of plastic grocery bags and some black electrical tape. When she got back out to the porch the wind was blowing hard. She could see the rain coming down across the field in large sheets. She faced Spats toward her so his face wouldn't get wet and told him to hold on tight, if they were lucky they were going to get to go to Oz.

Within a minute the air had turned cold. Hail came down and the grassy field in front of the house erupted in a million muted drum rolls. When it hit the house it tinged and pinged and Rose had squeezed Spats even tighter. Soon the hail turned to rain. The wind grew stronger blowing the rain almost completely sideways. Rose had blinked and tried to wipe the water away, but the porch swing rocked violently and she realized quickly that she shouldn't let go of the armrest. Then her grandfather's hat blew off. Her hair was soaked within seconds. She kept telling Spats to hang on, that they were about to go to Oz.

She saw the lights of the truck coming down the drive. She could make out her father running from the barn to the truck to assist her mother. She remembered that she could make out his ropey muscles in his neck and arms even when he was some distance off, even through the storm. Her father had grabbed the parcels from the back seat and he and her mother ran toward the house. When her mother saw her there, hair soaked, she yelled at her to come inside. Rose, quite calmly, yelled over the noise of the storm that she and Spats were going to Oz, and for them not to worry. Her father passed the parcels to her mother and grabbed Rose as if she weighed nothing and carried her in.

The storm was muted inside the house. It no longer seemed to contain the Oz-transporting power it held outside. So Rose and Spats continued to watch from the window, listening to the porch swing BANG, BANG, BANG, up against the house.

BANG.

BANG.

BANG!

Rose sat up. She was momentarily disoriented. Somebody was banging on the window of the car. The dashboard on the car read 5:45. Shit. She rolled down the window. A traffic cop with a mini waterfall pouring off the brim of his hat barked, "Move it lady, or we'll tow ya. This is rush hour don't you know."

When Rose pulled into the driveway at home, she could see Jim paying the pizza guy.

"What happened to you?" asked Jim when Rose dashed into the house.

"Fell asleep in the car."

"Seriously? I was worried. I called June."

"You called June, what for?"

"Like I said, I was worried. You are always home before five. There was nothing to eat so I ordered pizza."

"Jesus, is that your solution to cooking, pizza?"

"What's wrong with you? I'm not the one who fell asleep in the car."

"Can I get some money for groceries?"

"Sure. What's wrong with you? Didn't you get your new shoes?"

"No," said Rose, looking down at the floor.

"What, they didn't have your size?"

"No," said Rose, pausing, and for a second she thought she should just tell him what happened, but instead what came out was "They have to order them. Three weeks."

"You big suck," said Jim grabbing onto her hips, kissing her on the top of the head.

She looked up at him and smiled meekly.

"So how *did* you fall asleep in the car?"

"I don't know. I guess I was tired from all that walking around the mall. I just got in and I closed my eyes and...I don't know."

"Huh," said Jim.

......

They ate the pizza in the den while watching the news on TV. Tammy diligently removed the green pepper from her slices and piled it neatly on the side of her plate. Kiel was more interested in playing with his Lego than eating his pizza. Jim put two slices together, cheese-to-cheese, and ate them like it was a sandwich. After a time Jim would vulture over the coffee table, swoop down and devour the kids' crusts. Tammy called the crusts "pizza bones." Sometimes Jim would get up, like he did tonight, flap his arms and caw. Tammy and Kiel would laugh their guts out.

When *Jeopardy* came on, Jim cracked a beer and Rose turned to him.

"Can I also get some money for Tammy's skates?"

"Yeah, sure thing babe," said Jim as he watched Alex Trebek read out the categories.

"Great," said Rose softly, "that would be great."

......

Rose waited until after lunch, waited until she saw Vicki the bartender leave, then butted out her cigarette, got out of the car, crossed the street and went into the Scottsdale Tavern.

......

An alligator. A monkey. A red star. The Budweiser clock on the wall read three o'clock. Rose slipped her last twenty into the machine. Fifteen minutes later the credit display on the VLT read zero.

She lit a smoke and began to cry.

He had been sitting at the other end of the bar, watching. He now came over to her. He put his hand on the back of her bar stool and leaned around toward her.

"Excuse me Miss, but are you okay?"

Rose turned and wiped at her eyes with the back of her hand. She looked at the man. He was balding, slightly overweight, with a moustache. She noticed the red arm of the jacket. It was the man with the Detroit Red Wings jacket.

"I guess you want me to move so you can play?"

"Uh no, I usually don't play those things. I just wanted to see if you were okay?"

"Do I look okay to you pal?" sneered Rose, mascara running down her cheek.

The man paused, looked Rose in the eye, and asked her how much she had lost.

"What's it to you?"

"Maybe I can help you out."

"Yeah, like how, I've lost over five hundred dollars on this fucking thing. You going to give me five hundred dollars?"

"I'll give you six if you give me a hand job in the washroom."

Rose normally would have told him to go fuck himself, but it was the way he said it. He was totally calm about it, like he was asking to borrow a pen. And suddenly there was a way out. As sick and twisted as it was, she could fix the horrible mess she had gotten herself into. Hand job. Not nearly as bad as blow job, right? Wrong.

"Thanks, but no thanks," said Rose.

"How about seven?"

"Why don't you go down the street and find yourself a hooker, or call an escort agency? I'm sure they would be a hell of a lot cheaper."

"Cause I want you to do it," said the man calmly, his eyes locked onto Rose's.

"Why me?" she asked.

The whole thing struck Rose as bizarre and infantile. The man was creepy and his breath smelled like oysters.

"Why not you. You could say it was your lucky break."

"You're sick."

"Who just wasted five hundred dollars? People waste money all the time. You like to gamble, I like to pay for sex."

Rose didn't know what to say.

"See the waitress over there, last month she let me fondle her breasts for three hundred. Everyone has a price. Hand job. Seven hundred. What do you say?"

"No."

"Eight hundred?"

"Eight hundred dollars for a hand job? Are you serious?"

"Serious."

"How come you have all this money to give away?"

"I made a fortune on a dot com company. Now I have nothing to do but explore human nature," said the man smiling as he pulled out a wad of cash from his pocket. He counted out eight fifty-dollar bills on the bar.

"Half now, the other half when we're done," he said.

Rose looked at the money and thought about the ice skates, thought about her shoes, thought about what she would tell Jim about the groceries.

"Half now, the other half when we're done," he repeated.

"What's your name?"

"Taber," said the man.

"Okay Taber, let's go," said Rose, as she picked the money off the bar and put it into her purse.

......

When she was done shopping, she used the payphone at Loblaws. Tammy answered. Rose told her that she would be back at six with dinner and after that they were going out to get her new skates. Tammy squealed in delight. Rose smiled, said goodbye, and hung up. There was a young woman, looked like a student to Rose, on the neighbouring payphone. She was staring down at Rose's feet. When her eyes shot up to meet Rose's she covered her mouthpiece and whispered, "I love your shoes, where did you get them?"

"At Basil, in the mall," answered Rose grinning.

The young woman gave her a thumbs-up and went back to her conversation.

Rose grabbed her shopping cart full of plastic bags and steered it toward the exit. The blue of the lottery kiosk caught Rose's eye. The lady behind the counter smiled warmly.

Rose pulled alongside the booth and looked at the rows and rows of colourful scratch-n-win tickets.

"Ticket?"

"Could I have one of those?" asked Rose pointing.

The woman pulled a whole rack of tickets from underneath the plastic countertop to allow Rose to select her own. The tickets curled up slightly like spiny quills. Rose closed her eyes and moved her hand along the row of tickets, her fingers hanging down like a carwash curtain, just lightly touching the tops. When it felt right she stopped and snatched a ticket.

"I'll take this one," said Rose.

"Two dollars," said the woman.

Rose paid and headed off.

Just before the exit Rose spotted a penny on the ground. Rose picked it up and sat down on a nearby bench. She looked at her hands. They were still red from scrubbing. She had used Comet and a brush with rough plastic bristles.

The ticket said she could win a hundred thousand dollars instantly. She placed the ticket on the bench and held it firmly with her left thumb and index finger. With the right set of digits she clutched the penny, prepared to scratch.

For Rose, suddenly everything became very quiet. The noises of shoppers, their carts, their shoes, all muted. Her limbs felt heavy. She could feel it. She clutched the penny.

CHILIDOG LOVE

On December 20, Marvin McFerguson of the law firm Boyle, Goldstein, McFerguson & Associates, uttered his last words, "Oh fuck!" as he exploded into space from the thirty-fourth floor of Hartford Tower in the downtown core of Toronto. His attractive secretary Mary Donaldson, who wasn't particularly fond of heights, had asked Marvin to please not lean against the window, for it made her nervous. Marvin, uttering his second set of last words, "Oh yeah, well watch this baby," was attempting to impress Mary Donaldson by proving the structural stability of the glass window in their office by running at it with all the speed he could muster on seven gin and tonics.

Four and a half years before this day, as fate would have it, Leonard Kane had been suffering from a terrible hangover as he was installing the windows on the thirty-fourth floor of the new Hartford Tower. The sight of the food truck and Leonard's hankering for two large meatball subs had caused a particularly rushed and shabby installation. Had Leonard not been out until two a.m. the night before the installation with his good buddy Phil, watching the intricacies of Rhonda's pole-spinning talents at Cheeks Cabaret, Marvin McFerguson might have lived when he hit the glass.

Ironically, two floors down at the Christmas party of the law firm Bernstein, Doyle, Rogers & Associates, Paul Rogers, trying to impress legal secretary Susan Kay, was in mid-run toward the office window with a belly full of eggnog and spiced rum when he saw Marvin McFerguson, clad in a dark navy three-piece Hugo Boss suit, go screaming by on his way to death. That was the point at which Paul Rogers decided against proving the structural stability of the window.

That night when Paul went home, accompanied by his late night take-out from The House of Yan's, he turned on his television and watched *It's a Wonderful Life*. The film had such an impact on Paul after his own perceived brush with death, and in combination with the fortune cookie he had received with dinner which read, "You are the hero of your own story," that Paul, at the age of fifty, decided to quit his job and follow his lifelong dream of opening his own chili canteen.

Douglas Rogers, Paul's father, was a successful lawyer in his own right and had always pushed Paul to follow in his footsteps. At the sensitive age of nineteen, Paul had suggested the idea of going to cooking school. His father had exploded and explained that food was not something that one should concern oneself with, for food was the playground of the devil.

He went on to further explain that it was only idle and narcissistic people who bothered to indulge themselves in such things. Ketchup was only put on french fries as a lubricant so they would be quicker to eat. Boiling was the fastest and easiest method of food preparation, and constituted Douglas Rogers' entire culinary repertoire. No, cooking was no place for his son; it was a place for homosexuals and deviants. Paul, being a dutiful son, begrudgingly did his father's bidding and became a lawyer. Now, after fifteen years of clearing land titles, battling belligerent home office clerks, sorting out alcoholic ex-husbands and wives, and reading out last wills and testaments, Paul Rogers was free.

The first thing Paul did was acquire and refurbish a used french fry truck. Then he set to work experimenting. He locked himself away in his kitchen like a mad scientist and spent the next two months concocting and perfecting a variety of chilis. He concocted Suicide Susan's Volcano Chili, Rattlesnake Black Bean Bite Chili, Buddha's Vegetarian Tofu Delight Chili and a half dozen others. Within three weeks of opening his chili canteen, giant lines at lunch hour were a regular sight. The chili was a hit.

Six months earlier, Debbie Carlin, homemaker of three, had found herself out on her ass. Her cheating husband Ron had hired the law firm of Bernstein, Doyle, Rogers & Associates to represent him in their divorce. Brian Bernstein had managed to secure Ron with the house and most of its furnishings, the dog, and the most heartbreaking of all, full custody of their kids. Debbie was only allowed visitation every second weekend and one day during the week.

Bernstein had painted Debbie Carlin as a bad mother and a greedy lunatic who had only malice for her devoted and loving husband Ron. Nothing was further from the truth. Ron never spent time with the kids because he was too busy screwing his dental assistants at cheap motels. But the court ruled in Ron's favour and Debbie was left with pretty much nothing. Broken-hearted and broke, without a post-secondary education, and no work experience since she'd given birth to her oldest daughter twelve years ago, she took the first job she could get—running a Hot Diggity Doggidy hot dog cart.

Debbie went through the Hot Diggity Doggidy three-day trainee program where she learned grill management, propane safety and what Hot Diggity Doggidy friendly customer service was all about. Despite the incredible turmoil that her life had been thrown into, Debbie was handling it rather well. She missed her kids terribly, but found herself surprised by how much she enjoyed running the hot dog stand.

She was away from the mundane—the laundry, the dishes, the garbage. And she was away from her louse of an ex-husband. Now she was talking to people, interacting, recapturing her own identity. She realized that she had lost herself in Ron and the kids. In some ways Hot Diggity Doggidy had given Debbie her life back. She was becoming the Sausage Queen of Queen Street East, and giant lines at her hotdog cart were now a regular sight.

On August 15 at 10:46 a.m., almost six months to the minute after Debbie first got the sausage cart up and running, something happened.

Wearing filthy steel-toed boots, blue jeans, a T-shirt and an orange hard hat, Leonard Kane (the construction worker indirectly responsible for Marvin McFerguson's death) was standing in line to purchase a giant smokie and a can of root beer. At the same time Bessie-Gertrude Burns, age seventy-three, was driving down Queen Street East when she was horribly startled by the noisy ringing of her new cellphone. Her daughter Jill had given her the phone as a birthday gift so that Jill would be able to keep in close contact with her aging mother at all times.

Bessie-Gertrude probably shouldn't have been driving in the first place, and definitely shouldn't have been driving while trying to figure out how to operate a cellphone. But as fate would have it, she was. Bessie-Gertrude lost complete control of the wheel. Frantically she pushed all the buttons on the cellphone with both wrinkled thumbs in the desperate random hope that the damn thing would stop ringing. It was then that her car jumped the curb and Bessie-Gertrude confused the gas pedal for the brake and the car shot back across the intersection and into oncoming traffic—namely, into a big white truck with the words *Chili Willy* emblazoned on the side. Lives were about to change.

Paul Rogers hit the brakes hard and cranked the steering wheel. When the canteen truck spun around in a circle of squealing tires, the centrifugal force caused a tub of Texas Gold Chili to explode out the back door. It was like the truck itself was coughing up a large silver lozenge that had been stuck inside its throat. The lid of the tub flew off like a flying saucer and a long tendril of chili shot out into the air like a spider web. The chili hung still in the air.

To Leonard Kane, time seemed to stop. When it suddenly all came crashing to the ground, a small section of that tendril managed to land along the spine of Leonard's particularly tasty looking frankfurter.

Sometimes in life there are accidents. Sometimes they render greatness. This was one of these moments.

Shaken up a bit, Paul got out unscathed to inspect the damage. The Chili Willy canteen was without a scratch. His only loss was a tub of delicious chili. Mrs. Burns, on the other hand, had managed, with quite an audible bang, to knock out a parking meter and destroy the front grill of her Caddy. The monstrously tiny blue cellphone had flown from her hand and out the car window where it had smashed into pieces when it hit the ground. Mrs. Burns herself remained unharmed.

Leonard Kane stood frozen, looking in awe down the length of his extended arm. He was gripping the accidentally garnished hotdog as if it were a fragile holy relic. Paul, Debbie, Mrs. Burns, and a crowd of onlookers slowly formed a circle around Leonard. Nobody spoke. They all stood bug-eyed with mouths agape. Leonard looked with pleading eyes to the crowd for some explanation of the divine force that had manipulated chaos so exquisitely that it had managed to dress his smoky street pooch with a ladle's worth of Paul Rogers' mouth-watering Texas Gold Chili. No explanation came. It was then that Leonard realized what he had to do.

He hoisted the meaty jumbo to his nose and took a big sniff. There were several gasps from the crowd. One woman even fainted. Over the crest of the lightly toasted bun, Leonard's brow scrunched into fierce concentration. He lowered the dog slightly to his mouth and opened his gums wide. Had this been a movie, the soundtrack would have burst into a church chorus of hallelujahs when Leonard bit down. The camera would have done three-sixties around Leonard and slowly closed in and stopped where everyone could watch the big fat tears of joy rolling down his jowly stubbled mug.

It was magical. It was bigger than all the world's heartburn combined, and when Debbie and Paul looked into each other's eyes for the first time that sunny morning, they knew: it was chilidog love, and it was forever.

KILLER DOPE

Two Seconds tugged another can of Labatt 50 out of the plastic six-ring holder. The third beer was always his favourite—that's when he would start to get a good buzz on. Two Seconds listened to the traffic above, the whirl of tires, the monotonous pumping of the city's arterial blood.

Two Seconds looked at Little Fish working away in his jean jacket with a bald eagle patch sewn on the back. The ends of his long hair fell to either side of the bird's head, giving the eagle the appearance of Joey Ramone. The spray can hissed like a dragon as Little Fish put the finishing touches on the third UFO flying out of the eye of a kid—a kid shooting smack, languishing in the alley of a dark urban cartoon landscape. It was a landscape that contained heroin hookers and pimp daddies; glue sniffers and panty sniffers; Listerine fresh-breath drinkers and lemon Lysol inhalers. Most of all it was a landscape that contained fear. It was the best graffiti art, hell, it was the best art, period, that Two Seconds had ever seen. Little Fish had a talent. He was gifted. Man oh man could that boy draw. A natural.

Two Seconds liked hanging out with Little Fish, it made him feel special, like he was part of something important, something spiritual. They had been coming here, under the bridge, for years. They originally had come over to Hull as kids, as explorers on their bicycles, to fish and hang out. What kept them coming back were the cigarettes they could get underage at the dépanneur at thirteen, and then the cold beer at fifteen. Now they just came out of habit.

"Looks really cool Little Fish," said Two Seconds as he took another swig of beer.

"Yeah, you think so? I don't know," said Little Fish taking a few steps back, tilting his head from side to side like he was trying to figure out what he was looking at.

"No really, it's some of your best shit."

"I don't know about *that*, but it's not too shabby," said Little Fish as he walked over and grabbed his beer off a rock near the wall and swigged back the rest, arching his head and back until he was almost an upside-down U.

"Ahhhhh hooo-weeee, good shit," said Little Fish as he put the can back on the rock and stepped on it, crushing it flat into a silver medallion.

"You ready for tonight?" asked Two Seconds.

"Yeah, you?"

"Yeah," said Two Seconds as he grabbed another beer.

Little Fish sprayed a little more on the wall, then took a step back to see what he had done. He seemed satisfied, put the spray can down and went over to stand beside Two Seconds. They both stood there in the afternoon sun and looked out at the river. Little Fish picked up a flat rock and skipped it along the water.

"Okay, let's get this over with," said Little Fish.

"Right, let's do it."

The beer buzz was leaving with the afternoon sun. Two Seconds and Little Fish were heading into dark territory when they rounded the corner to the sights and sounds of Somerset Street. The hustle and bustle came upon them suddenly and snapped them back to a lighter state of mind so they could focus on the task at hand: buying a shitload of LSD.

Not only was Two Seconds a great dope dealer (the boy could sell a gram of weed with almost every pizza he delivered,) but he was also the greatest saxophone player Little Fish had ever known. Of course Two Seconds was the only saxophone player Little Fish had ever known, but that didn't matter. Little Fish intuitively knew that Two Seconds was great. Little Fish called Sammy "Two Second Sammy," or just "Two Seconds," because Sammy once said he was always two seconds ahead of the music when he played.

"I'm like the engine of the train, right, and the music is the caboose at the back. Follow what I'm saying? I'm always two seconds ahead of myself," Sammy had told Little Fish.

Little Fish got his name from his great-grandfather, a Naskapi Indian whom Little Fish had only met once on a re-serve in northern Quebec. His great-grandfather had taken him fishing. Little Fish had managed to haul in two dozen sunfish within three hours.

Two Seconds and Little Fish bobbed and weaved through the fruit and vegetable stands of Chinatown's sidewalks. As he watched an old Chinese lady root around in a box of green snake beans, Little Fish reached into the back pocket of his jeans and felt the cold switchblade he had brought just in case.

You never know. They were off to see the Fin, the six-feet-four hillbilly biker who was covered in tattoos and always smelled like Jack Daniel's. The Fin was a dope dealer and felon, and Little Fish didn't trust him any further than he could throw him down a flight of stairs. But the Fin had some of the best acid in the city and the dream was starting to become a reality—they were going to move to Tokyo. Two Seconds had told Little Fish that the Japanese took their jazz as serious as their sushi, and boy oh boy you've got to love a country that digs sucking raw fish. Two Seconds was going to play saxophone in the Blue Note jazz club, and Little Fish was going to teach English to little corporate yahoos all wearing identical suits.

After high school Little Fish had gone to the local community college and graduated with top honours in a three-year English program. Two Seconds never made it through grade eleven, despite his music teacher's encouragement. Still, between selling pot and acid, a part-time pizza delivery job and playing three nights a week at Casey's Lounge, Two Seconds made out alright.

They were off to pick up two thousand hits of purple micro-dot from the Fin. Little Fish had the six grand in a softball-sized bundle wrapped with a tidy elastic band.

The Fin ran a small crack house on Bronson Avenue that had white aluminum siding and a collapsing wooden front porch, like a giant mummy's head with rotting teeth. It was oddly misplaced between an auto repair shop and a ratty twelve-storey brick apartment building filled with wide-eyed new immigrants, beer-swilling college students, down-and-out pensioners and chronic welfare cases. The Fin's Harley was parked in the narrow drive. Upon sight of the place Two Seconds shot Little Fish a glance that said, *What the fuck are we doing here?* Little Fish just raised his eyebrows and smiled as if to say, *I know, but we got to do it, this is our ticket out.*

Two Seconds was about to hit the doorbell when Little Fish grabbed his hand.

"Friends knock, all others ring," said Little Fish.

They heard the sliding of bolts on the other side of the door. The Fin opened the door slightly and stuck out his greasy mug wearing a shark smile; like Jack Nicholson out of *The Shining.* His teeth were yellow and his gums receded far up giving the Fin a creepy skeletal look.

"Heeeeeeeeeeeeeere's Johnny" squealed the Fin.

"Come on Fin, quit screwing around and let us in," said Little Fish.

"Who's the cotton picker?"

"This is Sammy and he doesn't want to be called that," said Little Fish.

"What then? *Nigger?*"

Things went still. Little Fish and Two Seconds didn't know if the Fin was being serious.

"Yeah, that's right honky-tonk man," said Two Seconds with some jest in his voice.

The door opened wide and the Fin stepped through. He was large. He wore ratty jeans and a black Guns N' Roses concert T-shirt, and he had enough tattoos to cover the Sistine Chapel.

"Motherfucker, what did you say?" asked the Fin who glared with bugged-out eyes at Two Seconds.

Little Fish stepped between the two, said *Take it easy,* and placed a hand on the Fin's chest. The Fin slapped the hand away and moved closer to Sammy, who had already backed up.

"I want to know what this motherfucker said," yelled the Fin.

"I don't like being called a nigger," said Two Seconds calmly but firmly.

"I don't like niggers and I don't like doing business with 'em, got it motherfucker!" yelled the Fin while pointing at Two Seconds, his index finger poised in the air like the head of a serpent about to strike a mouse.

"Take it easy Fin, let's not get off on a bad foot eh, let's just do this and we'll get out of your hair," said Little Fish holding up the softball-sized wad of cash for the Fin to see.

The Fin looked at the money, and then looked at Little Fish.

"Okay, but he stays outside," said the Fin.

"He comes too or we don't do this," said Little Fish still holding up the money like a juicy worm on a hook.

"Okay little Apache, you and your friend of ethnic origins follow me."

They went inside. The Fin locked the door's two big bolts behind them; Two Seconds sensed immediately that there was somebody else there. The house smelled like must and corn chips. As they went through the narrow hall that led to the kitchen, they passed two long narrow rooms without doors. The walls of the first room were panelled in imitation wood and there was an old blue couch that had seen a million asses, a brown vinyl La-Z-Boy with the stuffing coming out of both arms, and a glass coffee table with heaping ashtrays and used hypodermics.

The second room had holes in the dirty grey walls and a bare light bulb hung down on a long wire. On the floor was a soiled mattress. On the mattress there was a girl slumped up against the wall. Her bony legs lay spread wide apart. She was not wearing any underwear. On the inside of both thighs she had homemade blue tattoos that read like road signs; if you followed the arrows pointing toward her cunt you would arrive in the township of *Fuck here*. Her eyes were hollow. Her bones seemed bigger than her flesh.

"That's Rita, you can both fuck her later if you want," the Fin stated matter-of-factly as they walked past the second room and moved into the kitchen.

Little Fish and Two Seconds didn't say anything. They just followed the Fin. Two Seconds knew it was there before he saw it; on the grey card table there was a silver semi-automatic pistol.

"You guys want to smoke a spliff?" asked the Fin as he opened a cupboard and pulled out a small Ziploc of weed.

"Nah, we just want the acid," said Little Fish.

The Fin picked up the gun and tucked it into the front of his jeans and very casually asked, "What's the hurry?"

"No hurry Fin, we just want to do this."

"Hey, what's the problem? I'm just talking about a little spliff. It's like you guys don't want to be my friends. We friends ain't we?" questioned the Fin as he threw a big tree-trunk arm around the shoulders of Little Fish.

There was a pause. The putrid smell of the Fin's armpit engulfed Little Fish.

"Yeah, we're friends Fin," said Little Fish.

"Okay, you roll," snapped the Fin as he threw the weed and rolling papers at Two Seconds.

Two Seconds sat down at the card table. Within a minute he had rolled a beautiful tight joint, thick as a Marlon Brando mov-ie cigarette. Two Seconds passed it to the Fin who inspected it like a predator would its prey. The Fin pulled his eyes off the joint and locked them onto Two Seconds.

"Very nice, Samuel," purred the Fin and he slipped the whole thing into his mouth and pulled it back out like a tampon between his lizard lips, getting it nice and wet. He fired it up.

They passed the joint around. Little Fish managed to squirm out from under the Fin's arm. The smoke curled and twisted in the air like the apparitions of tormented souls.

"Okay, let's do this," said Little Fish when the joint was smoked almost into nothingness between the Fin's dark yellow fingers.

"Always in a rush," replied the Fin as he dropped what was left of the tiny roach into a small blackened ashtray by the kitchen sink.

The Fin's actions seemed slow and very deliberate to Little Fish, like he was acting out the role of being a drug dealer and not actually being one. Little Fish wanted out. After this, no more psychotics, no more bullshit, he thought. Just this one last score, then Japan.

"We gotta meet a friend," said Two Seconds.

"Maybe meet your maker?" asked the Fin as he pulled the gun from his jeans and pointed it at Two Seconds.

Two Seconds didn't move.

"Whoa WHOA!" yelled Little Fish sticking out his palms trying to say that everything was cool.

Then everything stalled; time decided to take a holiday. Everything just hung there, waiting. No ticks or tocks, just suspended animation. Everyone wore the room's weight like a thick fur coat. Finally time came rushing back. The Fin took his gun off Two Seconds and started laughing like all this was the funniest thing in the world. The laughter was twisted and seemed to echo from a dark place within the Fin's shark guts.

"Okay, okay, I'll get you boys some acid," giggled the Fin as he put the gun back down his pants and opened the kitchen cupboard again. The Fin pulled out another Ziploc and passed it to Little Fish.

"There you go, that's six grand," stated the Fin, sounding like a salesman in a furniture showroom.

"What the fuck is this? This is blotter, we wanted micro-dot. I thought we had a deal for purple micro-dot?"

"My supplier ran out, but don't worry, this stuff is better than the micro-dot anyways. It's camouflage. The raver kids will love the shit."

"What the fuck is camouflage?" asked Two Seconds.

"This is what it is," said Little Fish and threw the Ziploc over so Two Seconds could have a look.

"A guy makes it down in Santa Fe, New Mexico. He apparently is one of the best in the US of A. Top-notch shit."

"You mean you haven't even tried it?" asked Little Fish.

"Trust me, it's good. Give me the money," demanded the Fin extending his palm out.

"How many sheets are here?" asked Two Seconds opening the Ziploc.

"Twenty. Now pay up. Come on, gimme."

"Yeah, well I count only fifteen. And that's only fifteen hundred hits, and there is no way this blotter is better than the micro-dot."

"The price is six grand," said the Fin as he rested his hand on the handle of the gun.

Both Little Fish and Two Seconds were tough kids, but not this tough. The Fin was a different breed. The hardware in his skull had soaked up years of dope and hate and was now a crystallized sponge, a poisonous sea anemone.

Two Seconds watched another drop of sweat roll slowly, like glue, down the Fin's face. The gun quivered ever so slightly in the Fin's hand, like he was holding a squirming rat.

"Like what are you going to do, kill us?" asked Two Seconds with as much confidence and sarcasm as he could muster.

"Fucking little niggers," yelled the Fin pulling the gun from his waist toward Two Seconds' head, firing twice.

Before the second shot rang out, Little Fish had the switch-blade out and flicked it open. He went at the Fin. Before the Fin could get off a third shot, Little Fish had jabbed the knife into the Fin's jugular and pulled it out.

The Fin spun around. Blood shot across the kitchen from his neck and sprayed the wall. Little Fish went at him again. With one hand he grabbed the Fin's wrist, keeping the gun away. With his other hand Little Fish stabbed at the Fin's gut. They locked eyes. The Fin's eyes were as black as a great white shark's. They danced like a pair of Frankensteins as the blood rhythmically shot from the Fin's neck like a water sprinkler on a golf green.

Then a cracking sound as Two Seconds hit the Fin in the back of the head with a wooden kitchen chair. The gun fell from the Fin's hand. Little Fish fell over backwards taking the Fin with him like a blanket. The Fin gurgled and convulsed, then went completely still.

"Fucking asshole, get the fuck off of me!" yelled Little Fish as he squirmed underneath the hefty weight of the Fin's corpse.

Two Seconds helped roll the body off.

"You okay?" asked Two Seconds.

Little Fish kicked wildly with his feet and slid back on his ass until he reached the kitchen wall. "Fuck! Fuck, fuck, fuck!" chimed Little Fish, visibly shaking.

"You okay?" repeated Two Seconds.

"No fuck! I'm NOT fucking okay!"

Two Seconds didn't say anything, he just absorbed the words. They rarely fought.

"Sorry," said Little Fish.

"Forget about it."

"I thought the bastard had gotten you. It happened so fast."

"The motherfucker completely missed. I was two seconds ahead of those bullets too," bubbled Two Seconds, trying to add levity.

"Good thing. . ." said Little Fish and abruptly stopped to listen to the faint sounds of sirens wailing in the background.

"Cops?" asked Two Seconds.

"Maybe. Seems way too quick. Who would call the cops anyway, that could have easily been mistaken for motorcycle backfire."

Then it hit them both at the same time when they looked at the kitchen wall: Rita. The sirens were getting louder. Two Seconds stepped over the lake of blood that was forming and grabbed the gun. Little Fish got up and nodded toward the door. Two Seconds went fast out the door and into the first bedroom holding out the gun, not sure what he would do or what he would find. The sirens were real loud now, coming down the street. He stepped into the room with Little Fish close behind in the hallway. There was Rita, still slumped up against the wall. Except now there was a red hole where Rita's left eye had been earlier in the evening.

"The bastard managed to miss me and get one through the wall," said Two Seconds.

"Ooooh shit," droned Little Fish.

The sirens passed the house and began to fade into the distance.

"Poor bitch never had no luck," said Two Seconds as he continued to stare at the bony tattooed crack whore.

"Anyone upstairs?" asked Little Fish.

"Don't think so," said Two Seconds.

"I'll double check."

Little Fish came back down and announced that the place was clear.

"What should we do?" asked Little Fish

"Let's get the fuck outta here is what we should do."

"Hang on a minute, let's think about this for a second."

"Fuck that, let's get outta here."

"The Fin has biker friends, Hells Angels. Big mean bastards. I'm pretty sure that's where he gets his stuff. Crack, coke, heroin, this much acid, for sure it's the Angels."

"So what are you saying?"

"I'm saying that if we leave this and they find the bodies, I don't want an Angel showing up at my doorstep."

"And how's that going to happen?"

"They ask around, they find out who is selling camouflage acid—ironically the stuff *stands out*—and the next thing you know we're in deep shit."

"I say we get the fuck out, like right fucking now. Fuck the acid, leave it here."

Two Seconds didn't like hanging around. But he trusted Little Fish. Little Fish had always given him good advice, for the most part. This was to be their last run before they had enough cash to put them well into the clear. Tokyo was only a few more grand away. The thought of slinging pizzas for another six months was killing Two Seconds. He watched as Little Fish paced up and down the hall rubbing his chin like a philosopher contemplating the cosmology of the universe. Finally his head craned up with a solution.

Two Seconds didn't say anything, he just took it in and digested Little Fish's plan. Two Seconds thought about playing his sax at the Blue Note in Tokyo. He could taste the reed on his lips. He trusted Little Fish, thought he was pretty smart. But transporting dead bodies around in the back of a station wagon was really risky. Still, Little Fish did have one real good point: no body, no murder. People don't look too hard for missing drug dealers and crack whores. Not even Angels.

"You think this is going to work? I don't like being in here."

"Yeah, but we got to move fast."

"Alright," said Two Seconds. "I'll get the wagon, some plastic bags, rope, what else?"

"Get a mop and some cleaning shit and get a couple of blankets, something to cover them up in the back. And get some duct tape if you have it. I'll do my best to clean up what we got here until you get back."

"We should move the bike so I can back the wagon down the alleyway, load the bodies out the back."

"I'll get the keys out of the Fin's pocket. Help me roll this piece of shit over."

......

Two Seconds was back in just under thirty-five minutes. Little Fish had managed to clean up most of the blood from the floor with the Fin's own shirt and some dirty rags he found under the sink. The smell of the blood had been overwhelming—iron, rotten foliage like wet decomposing leaves, death. Little Fish had worked through it. Had to. He wasn't going to let the Fin fuck them up. Tokyo or bust. They had had the plan a long time, and they had been working the plan for a long time. Sell acid, not crack or coke or heroin. LSD. Two Seconds had said there was a lot more money in crack. Little Fish pointed out that nobody busts acid dealers. Smaller take, but less risk; and you won't get hooked on your own junk. Slow and steady wins the race.

"Fucking stinks in here," said Two Seconds.

"Tell me about it. Grab some garbage bags and let's wrap 'em up."

They worked on the Fin, then the girl, mummifying the bodies in black garbage bags and silver duct tape. The Fin was a big bloody mess; heavy and hard to work with, whereas Rita hardly seemed to have had any blood in her at all, like she had been the victim of a vampire colony. They flipped the lightly blood-stained mattress that Rita had been on and plugged the bullet hole with a couple of cigarette butts and a piece of chewing gum. Two Seconds liked Little Fish's attention to detail.

"Let's put the bodies in the wagon so we can clean the floor up," said Little Fish.

"Out the back door?"

"Yeah, let's do this. Let's grab Chuckles here first."

As they both bent over to grab the body, there was a knock on the front door.

"Hey Rita, come on girl. Time to go," yelled a female voice from the front porch.

Little Fish held his index finger up to his lips for Two Seconds not to speak. They stared at each other over the bodies. All they could hear between the rapping on the door were their own heartbeats.

"Come on, hurry up. Open up already," continued the irritated voice. "I haven't got all fucking night here!"

"Hopefully she'll leave in a minute," whispered Little Fish.

"How about if she notices the wagon in the laneway?"

"I don't know, don't worry about it."

After what seemed to be an eternity of banging and yelling she screamed, "Fine, fuck you! I'm leaving!"

"Think she's gone?" asked Two Seconds.

"Let's hope."

They moved fast after that. Under the light of a huge fiery orange moon they loaded the bodies into the makeshift hearse and covered them with dark blankets. When they came back inside they washed and bleached the kitchen floor. But the wall wouldn't come clean. It was like the plaster had absorbed the blood like a sponge.

"What the fuck are we goin' do about that? We got to get outta here now," said Two Seconds frantically.

"I'll spray it with a youth gang symbol. I'll unlock the front door, make it look like kids came in and sprayed their shit around. I know some local gang stuff I can copy quick. We'll be gone in another ten minutes. Pull the wagon across the street where the Fin's bike is and I'll meet you there."

"Shit man, I don't like this. Just hurry up."

"Go go go. I'll see you in a minute," said Little Fish as he pulled a spray can from his bag and gave it a shake.

......

From across the street Two Seconds watched in the rearview mirror as two Angels wearing their colours pulled into the Fin's driveway where he had been parked only a minute ago. He spun in his seat and continued to watch out the back window of the wagon. He watched them get off their bikes and go up to the porch and knock on the door that was very much unlocked. *Oh fuck man, get out of there. Shit.* Little Fish suddenly appeared in the driveway at the side of the house while the Angels stood on the porch. Finally the bikers tried the door, found it open and went in. That's when Little Fish bolted. He ran like a track star on steroids. When he ran past the wagon he threw a big smile at Two Seconds and gave him a thumbs up, but before he got on the Fin's bike he came running back. Two Seconds rolled down the window.

"What?"

"Gimme some acid," said Little Fish out of breath.

"What?"

"Acid, LSD, gimme some of that camouflage."

"Why?"

"Cause we need to try the shit before we sell it, so why not now. My psychological state could use some altering in a big way."

"You sure? We've got dead bodies here man, is this really the best time to be dropping?"

"We'll find out, won't we?" said Little Fish as he stuck out his hand.

Two Seconds pulled out the Ziploc.

"How many hits?"

"Give me two, I'll play it conservative. You gonna drop with me?"

Two Seconds ripped off two hits and palmed them to Little Fish and then ripped off two more and placed them on his own tongue so Little Fish could see.

"Okay, let's get this over with," said Little Fish.

"Right, let's do it."

......

Heading over the King Edward Bridge to Gatineau, leaving the lights of the Ottawa skyline behind, Two Seconds began to experience the metallic taste of the acid in his mouth. The smell of the duct tape and plastic garbage bags grew more intense. It was fast working. He popped Miles D's *Bitches Brew* into the CD player and rolled his tense shoulders. In front of him, Little Fish, wearing the Fin's antiquated Nazi biker helmet (a single spike sticking straight up like a demented Teletubbie), seemed to be handling the motorcycle with ease.

When traffic slowed on the 105 just before the turnoff to the 5, Two Seconds saw the cars, the yellow jackets and the orange flash lights: a road check. There was no place to turn around, no way to get off. Two Seconds checked his watch: 12:30 a.m. *Shit, when did I have my last beer? About 7? Should be fine. Paranoia. LSD and dead bodies will do that. Fuck. What are the odds? Fucking road check tonight. Unbelievable.*

As Two Seconds watched a cop talk to Little Fish on the Fin's bike, another cop approached the wagon. Two Seconds turned down the music and rolled down his window. The metallic taste was strong. The smell of blood engulfed his nose.

"Bonjour," buzzed the big cop with the yellow jacket and the thick black moustache, like a giant honeybee.

"Hello."

"You English yes?"

"Yes."

"Have you been drinking tonight?"

"I had a beer about 7."

"Sorry, you had about seven beers?"

"No, I had some beers this afternoon, but not since 7 p.m. No beer since 7," said Two Seconds pointing at his watch.

"No beer. Anything else?"

"No."

"You look familiar, yes? I know you. You live around here?"

"Live in the city, just going up to my friend's cottage."

"Somewhere I've seen you."

"Don't know."

"You work where?"

"I deliver pizza and play sax at Casey's Lounge."

"Dat's it. I've seen you dere. I'm a big jazz fan. Big big. You're very good."

"Well thanks..." Suddenly, from the back of the wagon the muffled high pitched electronic opening notes of Beethoven's Fifth Symphony began to ring out. The big cop flashed his torch to the blankets in the back of the wagon.

"Forgot to turn off my cellphone," said Two Seconds thinking fast.

"You want to answer dat?"

"Nah, it will stop in a minute. I'm on vacation, no more calls for me."

"What you have back dere?" asked the cop motioning with his light.

"Camping stuff."

The distinctive opening notes of the Beethoven's Fifth kept rising up from the blankets like a shark from the depths. Two Seconds could feel sweat slowly rolling down from his temples. The cop wore some sort of cologne, and it was engulfing Two Seconds, choking him, strangling him. The cop kept flashing his light into the back.

"This your car?"

"My mother's car," said Two Seconds.

The cellphone kept ringing. How the fuck did we miss the Fin's cellphone?

"Okay, you drive safe. Have a good weekend," said the cop as he suddenly straightened away from the window.

"Thanks," said Two Seconds as he rolled up his window. "Hope to see you at the club."

The phone finally stopped ringing as he pulled onto the 5 following the taillights of the Fin's bike.

......

The still black water of Morgan Lake momentarily exploded when the Fin's motorcycle came bouncing off the forty-metre cliff face two hundred metres away from Little Fish's cottage. Within a minute the ripples had dissipated, leaving no trace that there had ever been any kind of disturbance.

Little Fish stared at the patterns the bike tires had made on the dirt path. He brushed them out with his Adidas running shoe. More patterns formed in their place—different patterns, geometrical patterns. They formed in the dirt; they formed in the grass. Intricate LSD patterns, embossed hieroglyphics rising from the ground. Little Fish felt the shapes' primordial essence, their being. He felt connected to the earth, felt connected to his people. "Let's dig a hole."

"Let's do it," said Two Seconds.

......

With the help of a rusty wheelbarrow, they transported the bodies to a small clearing deep into the woods behind Little Fish's cottage. They started digging. Worms, ants, beetles and strange winged insects appeared in the earth and on the grass.

"You see all them bugs?" asked Little Fish.

"It's the acid. Good eh?"

"Yeah. Totally."

For Little Fish the bugs slowly turned into large snakes. They oozed from the ground and over his feet, but Little Fish kept digging; they both did. There was no fear though. It was a beautiful thing seeing all those snakes moving through the patterned grass in the moonlight. Pale deer and wolves with glowing red eyes appeared at the edge of the clearing. They stood and watched. And the branches and leaves of the surrounding forest grew up toward the moon like a wreath made of thousands of squid tentacles.

As they continued to dig, Little Fish felt his fingers grow into the handle of the shovel like roots, becoming part of it.

And the great bird was there in the trees, watching. He felt the eagle rising within himself. He was transforming. The acid was strong, but clean. It had taken away the terrible essence of what they were doing, and replaced it with something truly spiritual. Little Fish felt connected to his ancestors, to nature, to everything. Out of his shoulder blades and through his jacket he felt the wings grow. He was becoming the eagle. He kept digging; they both did. For two hours.

When the hole was deep enough for the Fin and Rita to be locked in the missionary position for eternity, Two Seconds and Little Fish climbed out. All the animals, the wolves, the deer, the snakes, all of them with their red eyes backed up when Little Fish flapped his mighty wings. Everything was moving, expanding and contracting.

"Come on, let's get them in," said Two Seconds.

Little Fish didn't move, he just kept looking into the trees, feeling his own eagle wings beat, feeling the air move around him, feeling it all.

......

The sun was hot against Two Seconds' face. He walked through the woods, snapping twigs on the ground as he went. When he came to the clearing he stood before the fresh mound of dirt. He watched an ant crawl along the ground toward the mound of dirt. Suddenly the notes played. They gripped him with fear. He stood frozen looking down at the grave. Beethoven's Fifth. The tinny notes grew louder. A small bit of dirt from the top of the grave moved and avalanched down the side toward the ant. Something was rising from the ground. Those notes grew louder. Two Seconds tried to move, tried to run, but his legs were frozen. In horror he watched as the Fin's grey shaking hand emerged from the ground. The eye sockets of multiple skull rings around the Fin's fingers were encrusted with blood and soil. The hand gripped Two Seconds around the ankle. It started to pull. The Fin was pulling him toward the dirt, pulling him into the grave.

"Green Tea?"

The light shone brightly through the little oval window against Two Seconds' sweaty face. He bolted up in his chair. Little Fish sat beside him wearing headphones, tapping his thumb against the armrest. A small Asian face hung in the air. A neck connected the face to a blue suit and a Japan Airlines nametag on the suit announced that Meiko Tomita was the owner of the face. She was holding a tray with little white cups.

"Green Tea?"

"Yes please. Hey you awake?" asked Little Fish nudging Two Seconds with an elbow.

"Umm, yeah."

"Give him one too, please."

"Thanks," croaked Two Seconds.

Meiko Tomita gave a small bow and continued down the aisle.

"Five hours to Tokyo. John Coltrane on channel six."

Two Seconds eased back into his seat and sipped his tea. He looked out the window at the tops of the cotton-ball clouds.

"Little Fish."

"Yeah?" he answered taking off his headphones.

"Look at that cloud over there," said Two Seconds pointing out the window.

"Where, which one?"

"That one over there. That big one over there, the one with the silver lining."

"You're a funny guy," said Little Fish with a big grin.

"Yeah, maybe I am."

"Yeah, maybe you are."

"Yeah."

"You ready to do this?"

"Yeah."

Two Seconds smiled and put on his headphones and listened to John Coltrane blow his sax, blow that music loud and clear, the music that was carrying them all the way across the ocean, all the way to Tokyo.

ACKNOWLEDGEMENTS

Some of the stories in this collection first appeared in previous forms in *The New Quarterly*, *The Nashwaak Review*, *m-pty magazine*, *TransVerse* and *The Grist Mill*. "Killer Dope" was published as a chapbook by Bad Moon Books.

My first line of defence is always my wife, Marty. Her advice and editorial corrections, and love, have been simply invaluable. The next line of defence is my mother, Judith Gustafsson—thanks for everything, Mom. Molly and Henry, my kids, you guys are my inspiration. I have a tight circle of friends who have been reading and encouraging me for years: Jeff Hodgson, Henry Scott Smith, Brenna MacNeil, Ross Buskard, Shelley Little, Graham O'Neil, Claire McLaughlin, Marc-Andre Pigeon and the salon crew, George Sneyd and Susan Carr. Thanks for reading.

Special thanks to Byrna Barclay, Joy Hewitt Mann, Warren Layberry, all my friends and co-workers, Ian and Jim at *Misunderstandings Magazine*, the good editors at *Kiss Machine*, The Hungrymen, my extended family, special props to Mark Gustafsson and the Davis crew, and my in-laws Russell and Lona, and Susan. Two huge influences on my writing were my stepfather Dr. Wayne Howell and my good friend Colin Harris, who both passed away from cancer in 2000. Finally, my editor Silas White—your suggestions have been wonderful. Thanks for all the happy endings.

Christian McPherson's work has been published in *Kiss Machine*, *Queen's Quarterly*, *The New Quarterly* and *dANDdelion*, and in the anthologies *Open Window III* and *Seeds 3*. His writing has received several awards including the John Spencer Hill Award, the Ottawa Public Library Short Story Award and the Canadian Poetry Association's Poetry Competition. McPherson has a degree in philosophy from Carleton University and a computer programming diploma from Algonquin College. He lives in Ottawa with his wife and two kids.